THE SEMINAR

THE SEMINAR

REUVEN BRYER

New York

THE SEMINAR

REUVEN BRYER

ISBN 978-1-61448-192-8 (paperback)
ISBN 978-1-61448-193-5 (eBook)
Library of Congress Control Number: 2011945658

Published by:
Morgan James Publishing
The Entrepreneurial Publisher
5 Penn Plaza, 23rd Floor
New York City, New York 10001
(212) 655-5470 Office
(516) 908-4496 Fax
www.MorganJamesPublishing.com

Cover Design by:
Rachel Lopez
www.r2cdesign.com

Interior Design by:
Bonnie Bushman
bonnie@caboodlegraphics.com

For Riley Star, Heather,
Kristen, and Marcus

Never cease to believe that you
can make your dreams a reality.

TABLE OF CONTENTS

50 PASSAGEWAYS TO RICHES

ACKNOWLEDGEMENTS

This process of making any acknowledgements must certainly include the seeds that my father, Max Bryer (of blessed memory), planted within me. At a very young age I remember opening one of his countless books. It was 'The Iliad' by Homer. The book, written in Cyrillic Greek, had the inscription he added inside the front cover, '*Books are my treasures.*' I was also attracted to the fact that he used his beautiful skill by writing the inscription with a particular style of calligraphy, which he also used when doing freehand engraving on jewelry.

I must also mention my loving compassionate mother, Rose Bryer (of blessed memory). She loved, lived, and worked with my father, 24/7. I can recall observing with awe, my Mother sitting behind my Dad, feeding him nourishment from one of his books, while he sat at his bench repairing timepieces to earn us a living.

I have been blessed with many knowledgeable teachers and mentors in my lifetime. Listing them would probably fill this entire book.

There is a concept briefly discussed in *The Seminar* called the six degrees of separation. It explains our connection to each other through our friends and our friend's friends. It was from a seminar mentor and a friend that I discovered Morgan James Publishing. I am certain that I could not have found a better publisher on my own and have had a wonderful experience working with their team.

Of course I want to thank my editorial team of Judith Lubeck aka Momele and William P. Akin Jr. for their ideas, corrections, and creative criticism to raise the level of this long awaited project and help bring it to fruition.

INTRODUCTION

So what exactly is a seminar? Webster's dictionary defines a seminar as:
1. A group of supervised students.
2a. A course for such a group.
  b. The room where it meets.

It is also defined as a seed plot and a seminar is one of the definitions for the word: Seminary. There is of course no question about its relationship to the word semen, meaning a seed.

The author, having been a truth seeker since childhood, has attended numerous seminars, workshops, boot-camps, conventions, forums, webinars, tele-seminars, and institutes. He also lived and learned 24/7 in a seminary for a period of six years. Being a professional student or seminarist (not to be mistaken for a priest or an ordained rabbi), the author realizes that life itself is a seminar. Within a seminar environment, seeds are often planted and will require nurturing to sprout or bear fruit. A seminar will often teach some of life's concerns in a very short time span.

Along with all the practical, academic, and factual subject matter learned in a seminar environment, I have found that the attendee often experiences more than just the seminar's face value. It may not be as lofty as what the attendees experienced at the base of Mt. Sinai, like hearing the lightning and seeing the thunder, or the salvation experienced by those who attended the Sermon on the Mount. Something supernatural, often inexplicable, sometimes magical, seems to occur just before, during, and/or shortly thereafter.

The Seminar is a fictional novel about two people mysteriously led to a seminar called the Passageways to Riches and the extraordinary experiences they have, both inside and outside the event.

Although *The Seminar* is not a book on, or about any religion, the author makes reference to the omnipresent, omniscient, and ubiquitous G-D, while reverently and with awe abbreviating this name in various places throughout the manuscript.

Currently, the most popular seminars teach motivation, self-help, wealth attainment, personal achievement, success, internet marketing, and communication. 'Passageways to Riches' happens to touch on all of these topics and more.

The author anticipates that the reader will find drama, humor, mystery, and curiosity, stimulating the reader to take action towards achieving his or her own success. That action must include advice and help from other professionals, legal and entrepreneurial. One should not invest his or her time or his or her money without such consultation.

The author acknowledges having taken deliberate liberty and literary license with subject matters, timing, Biblical and historical events referred to within. All of the events mentioned are merely a backdrop for the purpose of fiction. All of the characters in *The Seminar* are the creation of the author and entirely fictional.

The reader may acquire feelings of actually participating in the seminar and have those inexplicable experiences mentioned earlier. Take responsibility and read at your own risk.

Enjoy,

Reuven Bryer

PROLOGUE

She woke up thinking, "Thank G-D it's Friday."

About to begin a three-day seminar on attaining wealth, she had no clue how euphoric, bone chilling, jubilating, and yet frightening this weekend would unfold. The wild ride she would take for the next seventy-two hours would be a series of events far more profound than any experience she could have imagined.

The actual title for this seminar was 'Passageways to Riches.' She had attended a wealth seminar once before held by a different organization. That previous seminar had a cost of fifteen hundred dollars but she was able to bring a friend at no extra charge. She brought Fred and split the cost with him. It took her two months to save up the seven hundred and fifty dollars in order to attend. She thought they had presented a vast amount of information and covered many areas of business. She received handouts and workbooks but never took action to apply what she had learned.

The invitation to this 'Passageways to Riches' seminar came to her via an email from an apparent affiliate sponsor called Enoch Enterprises. At seven, when her alarm went off she sat up on her bed and spoke to herself as she often does using her own mental dialogue.

The following is her detailed account of the weekend.

CHAPTER 1

THE TIME MACHINE

At times it all seems as if it were a dream. I clearly remember that morning when I was filled with doubt and occupied with reflection. I remember asking myself, "why am I going?" I spent seven fifty the last time and I haven't made a penny. Why bother? Okay, it's free this time but what is their scam? The last time they taught various 'avenues' to attain wealth but the only avenue I'm on is the road to psychological depression and doom. Life is so crazy right now. Tomorrow, it will be a year since Mom died. I can finally listen to music and be entertained. The one-year mourning period will be over. That didn't mean I could not be happy, but I'm not happy. Rabbi Cohen said that happiness could cure illness. He said laughing was like medicine. How could I laugh or be happy? He said that Mom would have wanted me to experience a great deal of happiness in my life but Mom was not so happy herself. The holocaust had broken up her family and separated them. From eight siblings, she had only one sister that survived, spending her life in an institution for the mentally challenged. Dr. Rosen thinks I should speak to a shrink just because I'm related to a Holocaust survivor.

All Mom really had was Dad, three sons, and me. Those three boys were a handful. Adam, my oldest brother, always got the attention. I had to be the one to serve them all. If I wasn't a woman I would be rich like Adam. He's tighter than a gnat's ass though. He wouldn't loan me the money to attend that last seminar. I think he would be jealous if I ever get rich and being so tight, he probably isn't so happy either. At least Dad loved me and appreciated me. I am his princess. I wish that he lived closer to me. I feel so miserable. I have to get out of this mindset. I can't think of anyone who would not want to be with me. I just want to know how to make tons of money. That will change everything.

Where is Fred? He said he was coming for sure. He is always on time and its eight-thirty, already. We have to be at the hotel at nine in order to get registered. I hate being late even if it is free. I know that the people giving this seminar are some of the most successful entrepreneurs in the real estate business. I wonder what facets of business they'll cover. How could they do this at no cost? Nobody gives away anything for nothing. I know that I wouldn't. People should have to pay me for my time; after all, I'm special. Maybe I'll meet some tall, dark, and handsome man there and he'll sweep me off my feet.

Fred finally showed up. "Let's go slowpoke, you're late."

When we got to the hotel in Manhattan, Fred had to park in valet parking. We ran to the glass elevator taking it to the fifth floor and hustled up to the lines for the seminar. The registration lines were long.

"What a bunch of suckers," I thought.

We finally inched our way up to the front of the lines to sign in. For some stupid reason they couldn't get it together enough to find our reservations but they said we were welcome. Thank you very much.

Everyone else had large printed nametags ready and waiting for them in alphabetical order at the tables. They had to hand write ours with a magic marker. This seemed so unprofessional. No sooner than we entered the room, some huge suit that looked like a con man bellowed,

"Hello, everyone."

He was average height, well built, spoke with a powerful voice, and looked like a con man with his slick spiffy double-breasted grey suit. Only a few voices answered him in a soft scream,

"Hello."

He then commanded,

"Come on everyone, you can do better than that."

The whole room then shouted,

"Hello."

"Good."

He said he likes a lot of audience participation.

"Thank you for coming to this event. I would like to introduce myself. My name is Marlen Gandalph."

"You must be kidding," I thought to myself. Is this guy a magician, a wizard, or just a con man? He probably changed his name from Merlin to Marlen so he could be perceived as credible instead of being named after one of the greatest deceivers of all time, not to mention he has the last name of a sorcerer.

"I will be your host for this seminar. To tell you a little bit about myself, I have written and published fourteen books on the subject of real estate. I have actively invested in real estate for over 15 years. I currently own over 400 pieces of real estate all over the United States, Canada, Costa Rica, Israel, and Manchuria. I am also an attorney having only myself for a client."

Everyone in the room started to laugh.

"That is not however what I do for a profession. I passed the Bar in 1987 after I graduated from USC with an MBA degree in Law. I am a highly qualified communicator and negotiator. I have been commissioned by various government agencies in the specialized field of hostage and ransom negotiations. I happen to represent several information schools and teach many different aspects of real estate, memorization techniques, positive thinking, healing, pragmatic mysticism, and self-mastery. I also dabble in a few other types of businesses related and unrelated to real estate. I can promise everyone here a fun filled weekend that will present a great deal of valuable information and concepts that you can implement into your lives and businesses from this moment forward. I want to congratulate all of you for taking the first step towards success by being here this weekend. That is what makes you special and separates you from the masses. Please allow me to begin by asking you to strap yourselves in and pay close attention because this seminar will be jam packed with a ton of information. It would be impossible to cover everything about real estate and the other passageways to riches in one weekend but I promise you and guarantee you will hear some of the best information from some of the most successful people in the real estate industry and other profit centers, globally.

Okay good, let's get started by my asking you all a question. Please raise your hands if you dare to answer. What do you consider to be your most valuable asset?"

The room we were in was huge and had unusually high ceilings with beautiful chandeliers. It was a conference room on one of the lower floors of this popular hotel in Times Square. Four aisles separated three large groups of seats and tables. The seminar was teeming with wannabe entrepreneurs. If someone at this point was to raise their hand with an answer to his daring question, they would willy-nilly retort, while most of the people would perceive of the person as unclothed and exposed. In drama school, I learned that public speaking was less desirable than suicide.

I was quite surprised to see an old man raise his hand. He was sitting in the center row of the three massive groups of seats and tables about five rows back. When he was called upon, he answered that his house was his most valuable asset. Marlen thanked him for his answer. He then asked the man if it was paid off. The man, whose name was Jack, said it was not paid off but he has been making his mortgage payments promptly, and added that he had some equity in the house since he purchased it twelve years ago with a thirty-year mortgage. Marlen explained with sympathetic body language and tone,

"When doing a financial evaluation there is a format that separates assets from liabilities."

This he defined as a balance sheet. He explained the difference being that assets were to be put in a column where money or something of value was coming in. Marlen then muttered,

"Liabilities were on the other hand, to be placed in a column showing where money was being paid or going out. If you are indeed making payments and not receiving any, then the item must be a liability. Ask any CPA."

This was a tough pill for the man to swallow. He claimed that he had invested his life savings from over a twenty-year span just to make the down payment on his home and never imagined or perceived of his home as a liability.

"After all, it was a lifetime investment. I think that the current value of my home is worth more than what I paid for it."

"Good," Marlen added, "However, the value is an opinion and it can fluctuate. Since payments are still going out and not coming in it is still a liability. I'm glad for you that its current value is worth more than your mortgage balance. Many people are upside-down, which is what keeps the banks and financial institutions in business. I will explain that concept later."

Another woman sitting close to the old man, named Dinah, jerked her hand up. Quickly called upon, Dinah stated that she owned a car with a mobile home. She had another year of payments on the car but the mobile home was paid off in full.

I was surprised that she felt this was her most valuable asset and Marlen responded,

"Good Dinah, the car still falls in the column of liabilities but the mobile home could be considered an asset, particularly if you were to sell it or to liquidate. Now, if you are making payments for a place to store the mobile home then it is a liability. The car could switch columns if there was equity in it and you were to sell it for a positive cash return. The bad news is when you are what is referred to as upside-down. That is when you owe more than it is worth. I promise to explain more about the concept of upside-down later on."

Another man, Jeff, raised his hand and when called on he claimed that his daughter was his most valuable asset. Marlen grinned and replied,

"That reminds me of my own father when he threatened to disown me. Folks, I realize that you love your kids but you don't own them. I suppose they could be considered liabilities when they cost you a fortune. Even though you can write them off on your taxes, they fall into a much higher category than financial assets.

We will have a break coming up but before that I want to give you all a gift that could transform you all into professional entrepreneurs and make you millions of dollars over the rest of your lives. Would you like that to happen?"

I suddenly heard a voice that stood out over the rest of the sheep screaming,

"Yeah!"

It came from directly behind me. When I got my audible senses back, I began to hear Marlen acknowledge,

"My most valuable asset is time."

He then proceeded to ask another question to the stunned group of wannabes.

"Are there any lawyers in the room?"

Two men and a woman raised their hands. Marlen pointed to the man named Sal sitting about half way down one of the rows and asked him, "As a lawyer Sal, in the calculation of your billings, what sort of time increments do you break down your charges for services rendered?"

Sal, the lawyer didn't disclose how much he charged but said he used tenths of an hour. I thought that was quite interesting. What nerve! The woman who raised her hand was Barbara. She said that she charged forty dollars for ten- minute increments. Damn, that's two hundred and forty bucks an hour. She added that the charge was for writing letters and yakking on the phone. When Barbara does her barrister work in the courtroom, she uses a tenth of an hour rate of forty dollars. Unbelievable! That's four hundred bucks an hour. Boy, do I need a different kind of a job. What am I thinking? I don't even have a job right now. Marlen then elaborated,

"People value their time differently. Some of us figure our time is worth eight dollars an hour, some, ten dollars an hour, some, twenty-five dollars an hour, and some, perhaps four-hundred dollars an hour. Whatever amount it is doesn't really matter. I'm going to make a point here that by itself is worth more than the price of admission," then he chuckled.

"I want you all to start breaking your time down into smaller increments regardless of the amount of money you place on it. Your time is precious. It is valuable and is the most important asset that you have. The only time that actually exists is right now. The best actuary or accountant in the world cannot do an accurate accounting for a time forecast, because who knows exactly how much time we really have. You can't count it because you don't know how much there really is, not us!"

Marlen then delved deeper into the subject of time, explaining,

"Folks, There is one thing that millionaires and billionaires can't buy and that's time. But, that's not entirely true. If I have to leave here from New York and go to Los Angeles, I can drive it realistically in about three to three and a half days. I could also fly by jet and it would take about six hours. Isn't that buying time? Not only that, but it would cost much less money to fly. I happen to enjoy driving a great deal. I drive mainly for recreational purposes. However, when I'm doing local business cross-town, I sit in the back of a limo and let someone else drive. The driver knows exactly where I'm going and has the route all mapped out beforehand. Being a professional driver, he'll know how to avoid traffic and other delays. While I'm sitting very comfortably in the back seat of the super stretch, I have a pen and paper, which I like to use for taking notes on any future publications and seminars. I also have my laptop to check any comparables on the properties that I am going to look at. By the way, besides this business of real estate, I also happen to own a fleet of fourteen limos and I get to write off my traveling expenses."

The audience started laughing and all I could think about was taking the time to have breakfast. Thanks to Fred being late, I didn't even have my morning coffee. Marlen continued,

"People, I have a friend who is a well known hypnotist and seminar speaker who values his time so much that he doesn't even use commercial jets for travelling to his engagements. He takes a limo from his house to the airport, drives up to his private jet without having to go through security, and is in the air fifteen minutes from the time he left his house!

You see, everyone is given the same amount of this precious commodity. We're all created equal. This asset is an amenity and there are 24 hours, or 1440 minutes, or 86,400 seconds in each and every day for all of us."

Just after Marlen said that, a PowerPoint projection flashed onto a projection screen. It read:

'50 PASSAGEWAYS TO RICHES'

Passageways to Riches #1,
Time Management

There was a quote below it saying;

"Until you value yourself, you will not value your time.
Until you value your time, you will not do anything with it."

—Dr. M. Scott Peck

"Folks, do any of you drive a car?"

About three-quarters of the room raised their hands.

"I realize that this is New York City, where public transportation is prevalent and awesome. What it is that I'm about to explain is another concept that can save you drivers something irreplaceable. To drive a car everyone knows you have to feed it. Put gasoline into it. When you do, fill it up! You're going to burn the gasoline anyhow so why not fill it up? Every time that you stop for gas, it takes an average of ten to fifteen minutes. If you add up all the times you stop for gas, it isn't long before you're taking hours and eventually days **TO GET GASOLINE!**" he yelled.

"Let me ask you something else, when was the last time you misplaced your keys?"

Everyone started murmuring and nodding their heads.

"There was a time when I was looking at ten to fifteen properties in a six hour time span. I had my property assessment list and the numbers were all completed beforehand."

I wasn't sure what he meant about the numbers, but I guess they are about the property values and offers.

"I had a route planned for the order of properties that I would visit. I would stop at home for lunch or just visit with my lovely wife and then dart out of the house to continue on my planned route. At this point, about three times a week, I would run back out to the car and realize that I didn't have my keys. So, I'd run back inside, look on the table, then the coffee table, check the door, check my dresser, then go back to the kitchen table, then the door again, then my dresser again, and everywhere else again as if some miracle would place them where I already looked. Sound familiar?"

Almost all of the sheep including myself shook our heads up and down.

"That event was taking me about an hour a week in downtime. In a month's time that is equal to half of a normal workday! Lost and never to be found. It didn't take me much longer to realize what that was costing me. So, I bought a key hook and disciplined myself to use it as soon as I entered the front door.

Another facet of this time machine is that in this period of the information and computer age, you are never more than 60 seconds away from anyone, or any place in the world! Remember everyone, the valuable strategy here is, rather than thinking in terms of monthly, bi-weekly, weekly, or even hourly, break your time down into smaller increments. The value you place on it will alter."

Just then, another PowerPoint projection went up on the screen.

> *"Somebody should tell us, right at the start of our lives that we are dying. Then we might live life to the limit, every minute of every day. Do it! I say. Whatever you want to do, do it now! There are only so many tomorrows."*
>
> **—Michael Landon**

Marlen sadly explained,

"When Michael Landon, the famous actor and best known from the television series, Bonanza, was diagnosed with that disease, which I refuse to mention, he knew he was dying.

One other thing about time management is that you can't manage time! But, you can manage yourselves."

All of a sudden, this guy sitting right behind me was making some bizarre noises. I turned around and saw him sobbing. He saw me look at him and I could tell that he was embarrassed. He tried to obscure his tears as I gazed at him. I'm not sure why I was so curious. He was wearing a black cabby cap and had grey haired wings covering the upper part of his ears that shone like goose down. His eyes were as black as coal and they seemed to stimulate a diabolical side of me. He had a protruding sculpted chin with bas relieved lips that appeared to be moving, drawing my attention to him magnetically, and yet holding me at bay. I was unfamiliar with this attraction since he fit no pattern of any men that I knew in any of my past relationships or experiences. When his eyes collided with my wanton gaze, my head repelled, bouncing back, almost causing me a whiplash. I didn't understand my attraction to this guy and wondered what it was that made him bawl. Then all of a sudden I could hear Marlen.

"Has anyone in the room ever bought a new car?"

About twenty hands were raised. He then asked if anyone had ever been advised by an automobile salesperson, to sell his or her old used car on his or her own, rather than trade it in to a dealer. A few hands went up attached to some faces with grimaces alluding to the fact that they had somehow been swindled.

"If you had such advice it was good. They were probably being honest with you."

Those same angry faces at that point were squinting and looking curious.

"Picture this," Marlen said with that wily smile on his face. Numbers then started appearing on the projection screen.

"Let's say you are trying to buy a new car priced at **$30,000**. You have a car you want to trade in with the notion that doing so will bring down the price of the new car. You also want to relieve yourself of the payments you're making on the used car. Your used car has a Blue Book value of say $5,000, which you would already know if you did your homework and were diligent in learning its value. The Blue Book, folks, is a general catalog of price values for used vehicles. It usually goes back about 5 years from the current year. Now, of course, used automobiles can be in many different states of condition. They also may have upgraded and more valuable optional equipment. That is also true for real estate property. The Blue Book itemizes much of this optional equipment and places a value on it. So the Blue Book is your basic guideline for what a used car is worth both wholesale and retail. This value is not etched in stone because prices can fluctuate when certain cars become more trendy or popular for whatever reason. Some will hold their value better than others. That will not necessarily be reflected in the Blue Book. You can also check comparable prices in your local newspapers for similar cars. Checking comparables is the exact same type of information process that we do in real estate.

Now let's learn some creative deal structuring." The projection screen lit up again.

Passageways to Riches #2
Creative Deal Structuring

"Let's say that you owe $6,000 on your used car wanting to trade it in for credit towards the new car. Remember that your Blue Book value was only $5,000. That in itself is the epitome of being upside down. You owe more than it's worth. Now let's say you would be happy to get out from under the payments for the six grand that you owe. Essentially you would like the dealership to TOP, or take over the payments. That would relinquish you from any further obligation on this debt. You want the new car and you now have two different objectives. The dealership would not mind having a potential $5,000 piece of merchandise added to their inventory but business is business and they are in the business of buying and selling both new and used cars. Their goal is to make a profit. Ideally, they want to, repeat this after me folks, Buy low and sell high."

Almost everyone in the room yelled out,

"Buy low and sell high."

"The person you are dealing with we will refer to as the Salesperson. In these types of negotiations, I highly recommend that you deal with a person that has the capacity to be a decision maker. It would be optimal to deal with a principal, an owner, or in many cases, the sales manager. You do not need an extra mouth to feed such as a middleman. The car salespeople in many cases know less than you know. We will still refer to this person as the Salesperson and this person is trying to sell and/or buy something, regardless of his or her capacity. This person knows that, because he or she was wise enough to ask, that you can't buy the new car without unloading your used car. Let me repeat that folks, wise enough to ask. Say ask, everyone."

"ASK!" everyone shouted out.

"Because, if you don't ask, you may never know! That could be a deal breaker. You then answer that you can't make payments on two cars mainly because you don't drive two cars and you only have a single car garage, to park that sucker."

I could hear that peculiar crybaby behind me bursting into laughter. I personally didn't think Marlen's remarks were very funny. Marlen continued,

"Now the dealership gets a formal appraisal from their used car manager in some cases. He happens to appraise it for say $3,000.00. Realize people they are not going to pay you a retail price, because they.....," Marlen hesitates pointing to the room and suddenly half the room yells out,

"BUY LOW, SELL HIGH."

"Wake up and smell the coffee," he says.

When he said that, I was ready to blow out of the room. Whatever happened to that so-called coffee break he announced earlier? My blood sugar level was at an all time rock bottom, my mouth was watering, my stomach was growling, roaring, and with borborygmus overtones. The last meal I had was dinner and that was only a plate of rice and beans. I was starving because Fred was too damned late for us to stop and have breakfast this morning as planned. I knew I should have at least grabbed a cup of java. There was a Starbucks in the lobby of the hotel and all I could think about was not being late for this stupid seminar.

Marlen began to explain,

"This used car appraisal was known as the ACV or Actual Cash Value. Now this information is confidential but the Salesperson has privy to it. The dealership is not going to disclose this information to you and in many cases they shouldn't. You're too emotional because your used car is your baby. The ACV is a wholesale figure and in many cases it may even be less than the wholesale value. You would probably storm out of the place if you knew the ACV that was quoted. The used car manager may be setting up a basic flip, which is similar to a real estate flip. He may have a wholesale buyer or someone that will pay him $3500.00 for the car before the papers are even signed. Now the Salesperson has you sitting in his air-conditioned or heated office depending on where you're at geographically. Nevertheless, you are quite comfortable. He will then write the deal up and ask you a key question. The Salesperson wisely asks you what your offer is. The Salesperson knows that whoever mentions a figure first, loses. If you begin by offering any amount, the Salesperson can counter with a better or higher figure for him. Whoever speaks first puts foot in mouth and that could be a very serious disease in the business of buying or selling anything. Now bear with me folks, we are going to break in a minute but watch this creative negotiation. Let's say that you agree to buy the new car for $30,000.00. For some strange reason he may agree to purchase your trade-in for the exact amount you owe on it, which he has confirmed to be the total of $6,000.00. You're done!"

I thought to myself, 'thank heaven'. I barely had the strength to pull my chair back, I was so hungry, but as I did so I could hear Marlen's voice override the screech of my chair legs over the tile floor,

"What just happened? As far as you're concerned you just bought a new car, right?"

This time I was the loudest to yell,

"RIGHT!"

"To the dealership though, the most they could pay for the used car was $3,000.00, which is what the used car manager offered with his ACV. Now hypothetically speaking, we'll say that the dealer invoice, which is the dealer cost on the new car, was $20,000.00. Even though you were upside down on your trade in, a deal was completed. Let's look at several creative deal structures the dealership made in their perspective."

Marlen lit up on the projection screen for all of us to see.

CREATIVE DEAL STRUCTURE #1

Cost for new car $20,000.00
Cost for used car trade-in $6,000.00
Total costs. $26,000.00

Sold new car $30,000.00
Sold used car, wholesale $3,500.00
Total profit, quick flip $7,500.00

CREATIVE DEAL STRUCTURE #2

Cost for new car $20,000.00
Cost for used car trade-in $6,000.00
Total costs. $26,000.00

Sold new car $30,000.00
Sold used car, retail $5,000.00
Total profit, buy and hold $9,000.00

CREATIVE DEAL STRUCTURE #3

Total cost for new car less dealer incentive from manufacturer for $500.00. This often happens when a manufacturer is motivated to sell out the product to make room for new inventory.

Total cost new car with adjustment....$19,500.00

Short sale to bank, getting a $1,000 discount for paying off the loan in one lump sum, which pays off the entire balance of the used car trade-in

Cost for used car with adjustment $5,000.00
Total cost both cars $24,500.00

Sold new car $30,000.00
Receive kickback from loan company
for the referral on the new car financing. . $500.00
Sold used car, retail $5,000.00
Total profit, buy and hold,
with some perks. $11,000.00

There are more ways than one to structure any deal on anything.

THINK OUTSIDE THE BOX!!!!!!!
SEE YOU AFTER THE 30 MINUTE BREAK.

While almost everyone was copying what was on the projection screen, I jammed my chair into the poor crybaby's table behind me to get the heck out of the room, so I could find a place to eat. I then apologized and asked the guy if he was a shill. He laughed and said no. I wanted to ask why he was crying but I opted to wait for a better time and place. Nametags were handed out at the beginning of the seminar which had large bold computerized print. They were laminated in plastic and were on small chains to hang from our necks. The name on the crybaby's neck was also hand written with a magic marker like mine. His name was Melky. At the same instant that I read his name, I could see him reading mine.

"Nice to meet you, Esther Malka."

As hungry as I was, I felt compelled to tell him that I never heard of the name Melky before. He said his father had given him his real name and Melky was a nickname that his mother strapped on him. Naturally, I asked what his real name was and he answered,

"Melchitzedek."

I assumed he was Jewish by the way he spat out the chitz in his name. Although the name reminded me of my brother's old Superman comic books and the cunning, mischievous, little imp enemy of Superman, who would only disappear when tricked into saying his name backwards. I also knew that Melchitzadek was a Biblical name. I now absolutely had to fuel up. On further examination though, I noticed that Melky was walking with a cane. I then finally sped off with Fred to feed my face.

CHAPTER 2

DUNGEON OF PAIN

Fred and I took the elevator down to the lobby. There stood a herd of sheep from our seminar, waiting in line to get into this overpriced boutique coffee shop. We waited about five minutes and couldn't help but notice the ineptitude of the uniformed employees who were lost, like ship captains gone astray at the helm of the cash register who couldn't seem to press the right buttons. We noticed a small Chinese restaurant across the street and so headed in that direction. Coffee was only a buck fifty and I was ready for my fix. Coffee, at half the price of that boutique joint. I also decided to place an order of Dim Sum, which was the closest thing they had to a breakfast meal. It turned out to be a small portion but it hit the spot. I learned that Fred had eaten earlier, which was indeed what made him late this morning.

Fred was actually Rabbi Ephraim Lehrman. He had been ordained only a month earlier, thanks to me. I had given him that push he needed to study hard for the tests he needed to pass. He only entered this restaurant to schmooze with me. Entering a non-kosher restaurant is impermissible according to Jewish law because someone might see him and assume that the restaurant served kosher food. We were careful to sit out of anyone's view; nevertheless, he wasn't allowed to be there. All he had was a coffee in a paper cup, to go. As soon as I finished eating, we barely had enough time to get back to the seminar. First, I quickly loaded up my thermos jug with some healthy tea that they had.

Upon entering the seminar room, the first person my eyes were drawn to was none other than Melky. At the rear of the room and closest to the doors we entered, he stood leaning on his cane talking to Marlen. I approached to within a few feet of them, and like a rogue covert snoop, I attentively monitored the conversation. There were others standing around when suddenly Marlen took off his wristwatch and handed it to Melky. Melky leaned his cane against a table and began to examine the watch. About a minute elapsed and Melky informed Marlen that his father was a watchmaker. Upon closer examination, I noticed Melky's hand begin to shake. He was trembling. The watch was shiny and sparkling. It looked a bit weird from where I was standing and then I noticed Melky's eyes getting glossy like they were when he was sobbing earlier. Melky's hand began to shake like a leaf and insisted that Marlen take it back. I was mystified by what was going on and suddenly Marlen put the watch back on his hand and raced towards the front of the room.

I couldn't take it any more so I asked Melky why he was crying earlier, hoping for an explanation of why he was also sobbing now. He had to catch his breath prior to giving me any sort of answer to my inquiry. He said his tears were tears of joy. As he spoke, his voice began to crack. He held his index finger up to apparently request a moment of composure. He finally began to utter that three months ago, G-D had radically altered his perception of time. He acquired some kind of infection, which he thought was the flu. He then got so sick and weak that he became bedridden. Two weeks passed before he could get to a doctor who eventually prescribed antibiotics. Shortly thereafter, he acquired another infection, this time in the gums of his mouth.

What had initially appeared as melancholy was now transforming into sincere joy on Melky's face. He now smiled as he spoke to me.

"After another few weeks of being bedridden, I finally got up to tend to an overdue task at my construction jobsite. It was only a few blocks from my house. The first thing I did was to pick up a small piece of trash no heavier than a screwdriver and felt a little snap in my back."

The contrast of Melky's subject matter was diametrically opposed to his expression, now a grin.

"I walked back home and went to bed."

Again, his voice began to crack and although serene, that layer of tears reappeared in his eyes. I felt very uncomfortable listening now but was far too curious to throw in the towel. He was now forcefully digging for words but described that the next morning he was in excruciating pain.

"For three days I had lain there helpless and with a pain like I never experienced before. After the third day in bed, I came to know what hunger and thirst was really like. I knew that I was actually going to die if I didn't get some water but I couldn't move. I rented this apartment because it was a basement apartment having tons of acoustical and thermal insulation. What initially attracted me most was not like most dungeons where decibels of sound bounce off cavernous walls and echo, this one didn't. Besides the fact that I am a home improvement contractor, I am also an R&B, Blues, and Rock musician. I liked the freedom to practice and play whenever I wanted, without disturbing anyone in the adjacent apartments. The insulation provided that freedom. The problem now was that I could scream, which I did, to no avail. My lips were dry and cracking from thirst. I was very hungry. I was now faced with the option to either die of thirst, lying still with minimal pain, or acquaint myself with a pain beyond my imagination and attempt to get to my kitchen for water and grab my cell phone. I finally went for it and it was Hell."

When Melky said the word dungeon, it somehow triggered a bizarre fantasy within me. Beside these real heterosexual impulses of affection that engulfed my entirety, I pictured myself chained to cavernous walls in handcuffs and just at that moment, I could hear Marlen telling everyone to take their seats. Melky felt compelled to finish and told me that in short, for the next three months, his entire environment was total confinement to his bed. I felt grossed out to hear that his bed was his desk, his table, and his bathroom. I sort of interrupted Melky and asked him,

"The watch, Marlen's watch, what was that all about?"

"It is the closest representation to a timepiece exemplifying the preciousness of time itself that I have ever seen.

Not only is it a Patek Philippe, triple movement, encased in an eighteen carat pink gold filigree case with I don't even know how many carats of diamonds, it is a relic that is a one-of-a- kind, probably having more financial value than a commercial property in Midtown Manhattan."

Melky then concluded, admitting that his father once gave him a Patek Philippe on his thirteenth birthday, his Bar Mitzvah. He said he lost it about a week after he got it.

"Even that one which was only an average Patek Philippe would be worth about thirty thousand dollars today."

Marlen began firing away with more BS, so we took our seats. Rattling away with more information, he apologized for moving so quickly, reasoning that it was because he wanted to cover so much information in such a small amount of time. He now proclaimed that he was willing to share any and all of his knowledge throughout this short weekend seminar. He asked that if we had any questions, we please wait until he called for Q&A, or we could see him or any of the other staff hosts at the rear of the room.

When I thought about the word staff, I turned around to see a line of tables. The staff consisted of about ten people sitting back there with computer software programs, books, and forms. It was at this time that I was quite certain they were going to try to sell us something. I knew there had to be a catch. That was their scam. My mind dwelt on what these programs were all about and for how much they could possibly be selling them. After some mental accounting and cumbersome multiplication, I figured out that if out of the three hundred and fifty people that attended, they would sell say, ten percent, or thirty-five people an information course, for say, fifteen hundred bucks, that would total $52,500.00. That didn't quite add up. These people affiliated with this seminar are involved in multi-million dollar real estate properties and other very lucrative businesses. That much I knew. What's a bubkus fifty thousand smackers to them? I did know what that would do for yours truly, so then I tried ruminating on some other formulas, trying to make sense of it all. I was suddenly startled to hear Fred's voice who was sitting right next to me asking Marlen a question. I must have missed about fifteen minutes or so with my cynical accounting evaluation and noticed that they had the PowerPoint projection on the screen at the front of the room reading;

Passageways to Riches #5
Buying Foreclosures

Passageways to riches #3 read Buying with OPM and #4 read Mice and Elephants.

Mentally, I had succumbed to the realization that I was totally lost once again. What the heck is OPM and what connection does it have with riches, mice, and elephants? Fred's question was how could he find foreclosures to buy? Marlen smiled and answered,

"It could take a day or two to answer that question more thoroughly."

He divulged that when property payments were in arrears, they eventually entered into a state of Lis Pendens. That is the litigation process.

Fred seemed satisfied with that answer when Marlen interrupted,

"That information becomes public record and anyone could find those listings at the courthouse."

Fred appeared a bit perplexed but I knew he was obviously paying attention and I could have him explain what I failed to hear about passageways #3 and #4 at the next break.

Marlen began walking up and down the aisles. As he passed by our row, I could see that he was sweating. I knew it. He had ulterior motives and ill intentions. His sweat was the proof. He said that the very last stage to the foreclosure process was when the property would be sold at auction right on the courthouse steps. He added that he in particular, rarely attends these auctions because he prefers buying foreclosures at a time when he could help people protect their name and their credit.

I'll bet! This guy is pretty high energy and I bet he couldn't give a rat's poop about anyone else's credit.

"Buying, before the auction actually takes place, also opens up the doors to do what is called a Short Sale as I mentioned where the car dealership offered to pay off the bank loan in one lump sum, asking for a discount on the debt."

Passageways to Riches #6
Short Sales

Short Sales were #6 on his hit list of the Passageways. As though he was portraying a saintly church minister, he said it was most important to picture yourselves in the current owner's frame of mind, and delicately understand that the people you will be dealing with may be in a sensitive emotional state in these situations. He then proceeded with his trumped up method.

"If you can gain the trust of the potential seller, and prove that you are, for example, a property deal transaction doctor, you might get a discount towards the debt on that which the owner is facing foreclosure."

Marlen then said with his wily smile,

"It would be a win-win situation where you can solve the problems for everyone concerned."

Yeah, a real mentch. Who is he kidding?

"You could save the owners credit by most importantly; satisfying the debt, certainly with a discount, buy a property which you will do only if you can buy for no less than twenty-five percent below current market value and with no credit check or dime of your own money!"

Even though I loaded up my jug of green tea with kelp leaves, aloe, wheat germ, and honey, shortly after the break, I was getting hungry again. Assuming that someday I'll become a real estate maven, I couldn't refrain from my boredom now. All of this jargon, like enough already! Let's get on with it, just tell me how to get rich.

As Marlen was going on and on, I happened to notice some guy about my age sitting in the rear of the center row. He looked really cute. He's certainly well dressed, not one of his dark hairs out of place, and tall. I'll bet that he lives on the West side, probably between the 80's and 90's in some lavish condo. I could at least see spending an evening with him. I cannot believe how horny I feel. It's hardly been a week. Oh no, what's this? Who the heck is the freaking redhead that just sat down next to Mr. Uptown? What a bummer, she's with him.

"Hey Marlen," I thought to myself,

"How about teaching Mr. Uptown 50 passageways to leave your lover?"

When I turned back around, I could see Melky. He was now sitting in one of the side rows behind me. I caught him staring at me. When we made eye contact, he turned away. I think he's too old for me. He does live alone but in a basement apartment in Crown Heights Brooklyn. That's where all those Lubavitch Chassidim live, centered by their famous 770 synagogue. He said he's been out of work for months so he couldn't have any money. Oh my, Marlen is on passageways to riches #7 and it's a different screen. Fred will have to tell me about all the stuff I missed.

Passageways to riches #7
Going into Contract

Thank heavens; Marlen announced a lunch break soon. I was starved.

"Folks, you now have done your due diligence and tied up the property, your deal. You know the FMV, the Fair Market Value from having seen the comparables, which are the most recently sold properties with similar architectural layouts and in a very close proximity to your potential deal. Verify with an agent or broker what the prices are on the comps, which will be your best gage to knowing the actual value of your deal. Remember you must ask questions:

Why are you selling?

How much do you owe?

Who are the neighbors?

When will you be moving?

Remember that if you can't ask for something, then you can't have it!

That is a truth in life, period! It doesn't mean that you will always get what you ask for but you more than likely won't if you don't at least, ask. Write this down," he commanded.

"The three hardest things to say in life are:

I love you.

I'm sorry.

Help me.

You needn't be afraid. You see, fear is just this:

False **E**vidence **A**ppearing **R**eal.

Get the contract signed. How much will it cost? –

As little as possible.

Don't leave more than you have for a deposit. You can use that cash to do another deal.

Don't put yourself in a situation that is irreversible.

Only no risk contingency contracts.

We do things like this, and in this order:

Aim   Ready   Fire.

Remember,

Before you invest, investigate.

You want to know your way out before your way in. The exit strategy comes first, understood?"

I was able to hear Melky's voice over all the others repeating after Marlen in loud support.

"Understood."

I believed he was working for them as a shill.

"Ladies and gentlemen, we have a lot of material to cover and I want to make a very important point here. What do you do for a living Bob?" pointing to some man in the first row who answered,

"I am a mortgage broker."

Marlen started to laugh claiming he didn't see that one coming.

"Can you learn all there is about mortgage brokering in one weekend Bob?"

Bob answered with a laugh,

"No sir."

"What line of work are you in Joan?"

"I teach dentistry at the Columbia School of Dentistry."

"Can you learn all there is to learn about dentistry or teaching dentistry in one weekend Joan?"

"No."

"Look people, we all need to find a mentor to learn from. Our ideal mentor would be someone that may have been to the school. Yes, the school of hard knocks. That is where I was fourteen years ago. I made plenty of mistakes and paid the price. Believe me; the price of tuition ain't cheap. It's far cheaper and less painful to have a mentor to stand right behind you to assist you when situations arise, and believe you me they arise all the time. One of your biggest obstacles will be your first deal. Once you take that first step, it becomes easier. Let's move on.

Passageways to Riches #8
The Bank.

Here we go. When do we go to the bank?

We don't!

Just kidding. However, there are some general rules to follow. Stay off the carpet. That doesn't mean you should burn any bridges to or from the bank. Stay on the hard floor as a rule of thumb. Believe it or not, the bank is a source to find sellers and even buyers.

Deals folks! Now, what do banks carry a lot of?"

Surprisingly no one answered.

"Come on everyone, **MONEY!**

In all of your travels and everywhere you go, you need to network. Always have your business cards handy. You may even have several different cards; I Buy Houses, Commercial Properties, and/or Real Estate Transaction Doctor. Some of these will do. Whenever you go into the bank whether it is to cash a check or especially to make a deposit, make it a point to say hello if possible to the bank president or another officer of the bank. If you are making a deposit, do the same thing that a male Peacock loves to do with his colorful feathers,

Flaunt it!

Realize that the more money that gets into your specific branch, the happier the officers are going to be. That's because the U.S. Treasury supports any positive cash flow to your branch with guess what? More cash, and that makes the officers look better to their main offices. The more those officers see you, the more support they think you are giving them. Try to build a relationship with them. It's all win-win if you play it that way. If they know you buy real estate, they can help you. You see, banks are in the money business, not the real estate business. The banks realize that non-performing assets are actually liabilities. When loans are due on properties and they are not paid, the banks are punished by the

Fed. If they don't meet a certain capital ratio quota, the Fed comes in and can close them down. That's right folks, you think you have pressures.

The father of the famous aviator, Charles Lindbergh, Republican congressman from Minnesota said, "The financial system...has been turned over to....the Federal Reserve Board. That board administers the finance system by authority of...a purely profiteering group. The system is private, conducted for the sole purpose of obtaining the greatest possible profits from the use of Other Peoples Money."

The banks do have another thing in common with us real estate investors. Do you know what that is?

WE'RE BOTH IN BUSINESS TO MAKE A PROFIT!

Now, the one thing we want to be careful with is who should be in the driver's seat? Come on now give me the controls. That's right; you don't want someone else limiting your ability, like a banker who could prevent you from making deals, do you? Of course not. You must understand that most of the time they don't understand what it is that you are doing. Funny, here you are trying to help them out and because they don't understand what you're doing they could be hurting themselves. It is truly ironic, but you absolutely must position yourself in the driver's seat at the wheel and with the controls. That way everyone will be happy with the outcome.

One of the ways banks shoot themselves in the foot is with the famous **Due-on-Sale** clause. What that means is when a seller turns over the deed; he must pay the mortgage balance to the bank or the mortgage company. That makes it complicated to take over the payments. However, there are ways to get around that. You have to think outside the box. Where there is a will, there is a way.

IF YOU WANT TO EARN MORE, YOU GOTTA LEARN MORE!

Contrary to popular belief, banks are not so rigid that everything is engraved into stone. Right now with all of the foreclosures that are taking place, many banks are actually motivated sellers. They can negotiate with you on countless properties. But, how will you know if you don't, **ASK, ASK, ASK?!!!.**

One last thing about banks and this might come as a shocker to you. If you needed say, a million dollars to do what you know will return a profit much more than that, how would you go about it? Well, act as if you don't need it! Yep, you might happen to say to a decision maker that you need advice on how to go about completing this sure-fire plan to turn a profit of x millions of dollars. Be prepared to show all the details of this plan and you might be surprised of the outcome. Cover your bases so as not to give away the farm in the process, but you will have to make certain disclosures. Try to understand this:

If you owe the bank $10,000, you've got a problem.

If you owe the bank $10,000,000, then the bank has a problem.

During lunch I want you to talk to someone on our staff. They are here to help you. Pick their brains. Ask questions. Come to know the team that we work with. Who is better qualified? Doing what others have already done can save you lots of money and even more important, time."

I knew it. Here's the scam. They want my money. I wonder how much it is. Baloney, what a waste of my time. I just knew it.

"Folks, it's not what you know that gets you into trouble, it's what you don't know. My friends, let's conclude with:

Contract only the good deals.

What is the risk, doing the deal or not doing the deal?

Only no-risk contingency contracts. See you after the break. One hour everyone. Remember,

Focus Focus Focus"

CHAPTER 3

OTHER PEOPLE'S MINDS

When Marlen dismissed us it was a little after twelve P.M. As Fred and I walked towards the doors, I saw Melky. The magnetism pulled me in yet again.

"Melky, this is my friend, Rabbi Fred."

" Sholem Aleichem, Rabbi."

" Aleichem Sholem, Melky."

"Fred is my secular name; my Hebrew name is actually Ephraim."

"Nice to meet you, Rabbi Ephraim."

I asked Melky if he wanted to go to lunch with us.

"Where are you going?"

"There is a kosher gourmet restaurant around the corner and they have pretty good food."

"I'll tag along, sure."

When we got downstairs, we went outside and Fred began walking kind of fast. I could tell that Melky was struggling to keep up with his cane and all so I decided to slow down and stroll with Melky.

"So, what do you know about real estate Melky? Have you ever been to one of these seminars?"

"Yes, I have been to quite a few of them. Over the last twenty years I would say I have spent well over twenty thousand dollars on seminars, courses, boot camps, and workshops on real estate and Self Mastery."

"You're kidding!" Fred, who was within earshot, turned around at that point and asked Melky why he has done this so many times before. Fred's inquisitiveness finally slowed his gallop down to a reasonable gait.

"Well, there are a lot of factors regarding real estate, other businesses, and of course, life. There are also many different perceptions that I feel worth learning."

Fred asked him if he had ever owned any real estate and Melky answered,

"No, but I have worked for real estate developers that needed my expertise in acquiring and developing commercial and residential real estate properties. I have also incorporated my seminar trainings with pre-construction planning and have been well paid for that knowledge." Melky added that the industry is always changing and it pays to keep up. I asked Melky how long he has been in the business.

"Forty years, Esther."

"Wow!, why haven't you done any of your own deals?"

He said he came close to doing a lease option deal and then chickened out at crunch time.

"That one deal cost me seven hundred and fifty thousand dollars and that was thirty years ago. I shudder to think what that money would be worth today. The kicker was that the owner needed to move to Chicago. We were in California. He was very motivated. I was leasing the property with an option to buy. He wanted thirty-five grand for this ten-acre farm. It had a huge four bedroom house, a one bedroom cottage, a one bedroom trailer, a third of an acre irrigated garden, a third of an acre orchard with apples, plums and walnuts galore, not to mention livestock, four bulls, an Appaloosa horse, and a bunch of rabbits. He couldn't take them to Chicago. That was a prime example of losing money by not doing the deal."

Fred asked Melky what he thought about this particular seminar so far and Melky answered,

"The information that we got from Marlen this morning was probably more valuable than I got out of the last twenty thousand dollars worth of seminars that I have taken."

Fred's eyes popped open wide and examined with question,

"You're kidding?"

"Rabbi, there was one single point made, that alone will change my perception and life forever. I know it will bring me to a higher level financially and soon, I hope."

We walked a little further and I wondered why Fred didn't ask Melky what that valuable point was. We went into the restaurant and sat at a table. It was a buffet style and the waitress left us some plates. Fred jumped up immediately and approached the food counter. I asked Melky why he wasn't married.

"I was married and got divorced seven years ago."

"How long were you married?"

"That marriage lasted five and a half years."

"You were married more than once?"

"Yep," he smiled.

"Twice?"

He just smiled and about a minute later, he asked me if I was ever married. I answered that I was never married but endured a long lasting relationship, which just didn't work out. I felt prompted to blurt out that I wanted to have children and find a caring man that could give me everything that I want. Melky seemed to have read my mind and asked me what I wanted. I told him I wanted the finer things in life.

"I want my man to listen to me attentively, to help me cook, to take care of the children, to wait on me. I kind of hope he has lots of money, probably to minimize those types of problems. He must however, be able to shelter me, occasionally buy me nice clothes so I can look good in his eyes, and just satisfy me."

He told me that looking good should be no problem for me, and then he asked if I could prioritize the three main items that I wanted, other than those I already mentioned. I decided to get up and find something to eat. Melky just sat there and then got a bottle of orange juice. He nursed that juice for a long while and had a grin on his face like a mule eating briars. When Fred sat down, he made a blessing over his bread. I then sat down with my food and Melky again asked me if I could prioritize what I was looking for in a husband. I asked him why he wanted me to do that.

"Perhaps I could help you. The better I know you, the easier it could be to help you find your Beshert, your soul mate. There is one person out there that is your exact soul mate. We all have one in particular."

As I began to eat, he looked down at my hands and remarked,

"I can't believe it; you have that same terrible habit that I have."

"And just what is that," I asked.

"You bite your pretty little fingernails."

I really didn't like him noticing that and became annoyed. Indifferently, he just kept that grin on his face up until the time we got up to leave.

When the three of us got up to the cash register, Fred quickly paid for his lunch and mine. I then noticed Melky open up his wallet to pay for his orange juice, which was all he ordered at the joint. It looked like all he had was three dollars in his wallet. He caught me staring at his wallet, got nervous, and dropped the wallet on the floor. The contents of his wallet went flying all around the floor in front of the register. I then bent over to help him pick up his cards and all. I took a minute to look at some. The cards that got my attention were a fire department certificate, a card with an official looking badge reading, Animal Abuse Investigator for the Humane Society, and a Rabbinical school I.D. The school I.D.

was dated 1990 thru 1996. I handed them to Melky while he paid and then we left.

We headed back to the hotel. Although I found Melky a little annoying, it was as though he looked at me with approval. Well of course he would. We marched back to the hotel and when we entered the seminar room, many people were standing at the rear of the room asking questions to the staff and then Marlen yelled out,

"Okay everyone, please take your seats. Much to do and very little time to do it in."

Bored, I was, but something about Marlen and something about Melky.

Passageways to Riches #9
A Plan of Action.

"Ladies and gentlemen, I'm going to pick up the pace now or we won't be able to complete this seminar. There are three basic laws of manifestation. They begin with a thought or a dream. Then you have to do what it takes in order to make it real. The last and final step is action or having the dream. The Eastern cultures call the procedure: Be, Do, and Have. Others refer to it as: Thought, Speech, and Action. Regardless of what you may call it, it begins with an idea, a thought, or a dream. Your thoughts are physical and all-the-more-so is speech. A thought can become a plan. Even if you feel that your parents didn't plan you, you were planned by G-D. You are not a coincidence. Every man and every woman was created into something from nothing. We were created in G-D's image. We have the ability to take a mere thought and develop it into something. Why not something of value?

A plan of action is beneficial no matter what sort of business you're doing. You see, those who fail to plan, plan to fail. A business is not a hobby, but a hobby could become a business. When you are serious, it is wise to create a formal plan. Do it on paper, organize it. Have a table of contents, a cover letter, and an executive summary. Describe what you are offering. Include a comparative analysis, and a sales plan. Show how it will be managed and include a financial spreadsheet, an appendix, and any other supporting documentation. Describe your business including the entire team of responsible parties. You want to show that you are well structured. Most of all describe the potential. How much do you intend on earning.

Some successful people have a plan they call Plan A. When they are very persistent, there may be no Plan B. That said, sometimes you have to make certain adjustments but stick to your plan or come up with an even better one.

If your plan involves real estate, be sure that you know your market. Know the comparables. Know what it will take to do the repairs. Know all of the expenses. Most important, know your exit strategy before you begin. Remember, Aim, Ready, Fire.

Okay staff, what's next?"

Passageways to Riches #10
Finding Money

"We have already discussed Mice and Elephants. Remember that if you are only with a mouse's capital, then you may need an elephant. Having one or two more mice may not get the job done. You will probably, but not necessarily, have to offer a piece of the pie. Having a piece or pieces of pie is better than no pie at all. Hard money is more expensive but so what. Hard moneylenders do not care about your credit line and you shouldn't have to fill out an application for credit. You will put up collateral though and the lender probably hopes that you will default. Obviously, if you default, he gets the good deal. Maybe you will have to pay 15% in interest and payable in six months, or a year, which is of course even better yet. So what the heck, get the deal done. Know your way out before you get in.

There is also a type of lending called transactional funding. This is using OPM on an even shorter term, perhaps weekly or monthly. I myself, and just about everyone I know, use OPM.

Yes, Other Peoples' Money is the least risky. My friends, the richest people in the world, get this folks, the Richest People in the World use Other People's Money. If you can convince professional lenders to invest their money, then you know you must have a sound plan. Otherwise they probably won't invest. It is that simple. Don't panic if it seems like a lot of money to you. In fact the more money involved, the more the profit should be. Ten percent of a million is one hundred thousand and the difference between 100,000 and 1,000,000 is **one zero**. Why Panic?

Excuse me folks, but does anyone remember what else I said about OPM earlier?

A pretty woman in one of the side rows darted her hand up and Marlen pointed to her.

"Yes Darla."

She answered that OPM also stood for using Other People's Minds. When I started wondering if Marlen was going to teach us how to read minds, he handed her a hundred dollar bill.

"Very good Darla, and who can tell me what that means?"

Darla darted her hand up again but this time he pointed to a man in the center row whose name was Sid. "Go ahead Sid."

"It means you can learn from and use the teachings of a mentor or mentors."

Marlen handed Sid another hundred and commented that we must be paying attention. I was upset that I wasn't paying attention. Coulda used that C-note.

"Folks, I have to tell you that although we are interested in any type of business, provided it's legal of course, real estate is where I have been the most successful. I do admit to having other avenues for wealth building but I happen to like real estate the most. Do you all know that even now, in a so-called slow market, everyone still needs a place to live? Check this out; in twenty-five years from now the population will double! That is a fact. Folks, I help people with money problems in real estate and I find homes and sell them to some wonderful, wonderful families. Realize that right now America is on sale. This is a perfect time to buy and more money is made at the purchase than at the sale!"

'My goodness,' I thought. How long do I have to hear this Saint? Spare me, he is a real good-deed-darling-mitzvah maker, isn't he? When is he going to ask everyone to just fork over his or her wallets, sign over their paychecks, and hand over their firstborn?

"My friends, finding money is a piece of cake. They print tons of it every day. If you think it's scarce, then it will be. If your focus is to attract money, then sources will be banging on your doors to hand it to you. Think positive.

Let's move on:

Passageways to Riches #11
Retailing Houses

Is everyone having a good time?"

Marlen seemed arrogant and over confident that we were all having a good time. Frankly though, I was expecting some far greater revelations about how to get rich, and none of this seemed to blow my skirt up. Everyone else however was ranting and raving about Marlen.

"This retailing market is about finding houses that are good to go. They do not need much work, if any at all. If you are looking for a project this is not for you. Besides, rehabbing can be like a j.o.b. In this market, the houses need maybe a tad of cosmetic work. The primary focus for this market is to get free equity taking over debt, like taking over payments that we described earlier. You want to control the house long enough to eventually liquidate and put cash into your pocket. I will explain this in more detail a little later if we have time. The price ranges are relative to your targeted area. A must in almost any market is to buy, how folks?"

Everyone yelled out, **"Buy low, sell high."**

"That's right, if you are indeed BUYING, but guess what?, There are times when owners will **GIVE** you their property with no money down, and/or just GIVE you their property."

Now I was becoming far more than cynical or even skeptical for that matter. Who in their right freaking mind would just give you their property?

"Remember folks, you're looking for serious and motivated sellers. In this present economy, I promise you they're out there. Whether they have a lot of equity or are even upside down, there is money to be made, and that needs to be where your focus is.

Along with that, let me say something that I find extremely important. To be successful using any of these methods, you will attain great wealth if you do it for the good. You must recognize the tremendous responsibility you have to your family, friends, and your community. This spirituality shouldn't be sacrificed just for the material gain. Remember that folks and I promise you will find riches. Charity and helping others is a darn good motive for being successful."

As silly as that sounded, I sensed sincerity in Marlen's voice, but was he now going to give a seminar on some newly concocted religion.

Marlen continued,

"You have to be self-confident. You are not doing anything illegal, at least, you better not be. This is another reason to have a mentor and/or, a good attorney. Do not be defensive. Be confident that what you are doing is good. Isn't making a lot of money good? How about helping sellers and buyers solve their problems. Building up your credit rating is just another great tool in investing, yet not a top priority. We'll get into that a little later.

Locating good investment opportunities will require some pounding the pavement. I must warn you that after you do your first deal, if you have never done one, this business can become addicting. Delegating someone else to do this pavement pounding can prove very wise. Your time is money and spending time with your loved ones should never be compromised. Besides, there are plenty of birddogs out there at your disposal. How about your mail carrier. They see all the houses on all the blocks and may be familiar with many leads. If you do use them, remember to reward them. The same should be true for bankers and realtors etc. They are just a few of the examples.

You see this is a numbers game. A good realistic ratio is for every 100 properties that you have on paper, you should look at 10. After you have culled out the bad ones, make three offers, and close on one. <u>Follow up</u> on any possibilities.

100/10/3/1

Know what you are looking for.
Know where to look.
Know how you are going to buy.

A motivated seller may have to move to the other end of the country. In that situation, the owner may simply hand over the deed and even give you time before you make any form of a payment. You would be helping him out and buying yourself time to find a buyer, or a Lessee, which we will get into later. Motivated sellers exist for a reason. Learn the reason and help them out. Here are a few candidates:

Pre-bankruptcy, tax problems, tax liens.
Not current on the market value or knowledge of the business.
Foreclosures.
Too many rental vacancies.
In need of repairs.
Relocation, transfer, retirement.
Live too far away to manage.
Divorce, litigation, or health issues.
Estate sales, inherited properties, probate.

Loss of job, pay cuts, stock market losses, loss of benefits. Substance or alcohol problems.

I'll give you one other tip on this subject since we don't have all that much time here to fully master this market. The more attractive this house looks at the time to sell, the better. The worse that it looks at the time to buy, but with a potential for making it pretty, is also the better. A simple paint job with light off white colors seems to be the most popular. Some attractive plants in the front yard are also good selling tactics. You can also get these pretty houses without even taking title. Those are called options or leasing with options. We'll get into those soon.

Passageways to Riches #12
Wholesaling Houses

"Not only should you have a retail buyers list but also be prepared with a wholesale buyers list.

Network! Tell the wholesale buyers that you happen to come across these deals periodically and you can't always handle all of these deals. Ask them if they can come up with the money and close quickly. What price range are they looking for? You can find these wholesale buyers at real estate clubs. There are many of these clubs in all major cities. They do the same thing you do and every one of them you should perceive of as a potential buyer and/or seller. Join one or more clubs. You can also learn from them. Is there a problem with you making a profit on a sale and letting someone else also make a profit, maybe even bigger than yours? Heck no! That might even alleviate the headache of you doing the repairs, or putting more of your money into them. The main difference is contrary to what you have already learned here. In this category you must buy low and sell low. You will have to sharpen up your pencils in establishing the value. You don't have to sit on these houses very long. In many cases, not more than a day. In the process of making the offer you will be well suited to follow this formula."

Marlen walked over to the PowerPoint projector and put this on the screen:

1. Determine the ARV.
2. Subtract the repair costs.
3. Subtract all purchase costs.
4. Subtract the holding costs.
5. Subtract the selling costs.
6. Subtract a fudge factor (4-7%).
7. The result is your MAO- Most allowable offer.

"The ARV is the After Repaired Value. You must estimate any necessary repair costs. These houses do not necessarily need to be so pretty. Your purchase costs should not include the down payment and that must be very low if you are making a down payment at all. If the holding costs are over 1%, then you may not have a wholesale prospect. The selling costs should not exceed 3% and that is without a Realtor being involved.

Passageways to Riches #13
Options and

Passageways to Riches #14
Lease Options

"Options are just the legal right to a buyer from a seller to purchase property at a predetermined price. It has to be in writing. The option must show the agreed to price or something else of value like perhaps another property that the buyer may wish to trade for this property being optioned. The only one bound to this contract is the seller. If the optionee, who is the buyer, does not wish to exercise the option to buy the property, he does not have to. This is called a unilateral contract. Now you may think that this type of contract only benefits the buyer, right?"

Here again many people answered,

"Right," but Marlen surprised them by adding,

"This can be a win-win situation for both parties. During the option period, the seller retains the ownership. The price of the property may be high or at market value. The seller may establish a price based on the rise of inflation during the option period. Any option money received by the seller towards the purchase price whether it is in monthly payments or in a lump sum, the amount is tax deferred. No taxes are due until the option is either completed or forfeited.

If the buyer/optionee decides not to buy, the monies paid to the seller are treated as ordinary income and he has control of that money, at least for a period of time. Also, if the rents are not paid on time, the option is forfeited. That's a pretty good incentive for the buyer/optionee to pay rent on time.

The tenant/buyer/optionee also has a pride of ownership and that is an incentive for him to take better care of the property. In addition, the rent could be at a higher than normal rate. Therefore, you see there are potential benefits for the seller/current owner.

The buyer/optionee can buy a property for an amount agreed upon at the time the option was written. What if the prices go up during the allotted time that the option is due? The buyer then has purchased below market value before the option is due. The buyer/optionee can also choose to walk away from the contract. This is known as good leveraging.

In the case of an option, it gives the buyer/optionee control. You always want to notarize and record a memorandum of option. Have all of the transfer documents held in escrow during the option. Protect your option position with a title search and insurance.

Now in a lease option the buyer/lessee gets the benefit of occupying the property and possibly make improvements on it to raise the value. And, he may choose to sub-lease it out. Here is the way I have done some lease options in the past. First, I found a motivated seller. I offered to make his payments monthly until I was ready to buy or found someone else to buy. I had my own lease agreement and told him I would lease the property for 1 year with the right to renew the lease each year for ten consecutive years or buy the property for the agreed price at any time I was prepared to do so. That was basically it, outside of the fact that through my negotiation skills I also got him to give me two months to move in or find a buyer before making a payment. At that point, after the agreement was made, I was able to sub-lease it to a prospect found in my database for the positive cash flow I was trying to achieve. That's basically it.

This is one of the easiest ways to take control of a property at the least expense. Folks if you are making an extra $100 a month per deal, how many deals would you need to find in order to give you a decent positive cash flow while you are doing other deals or finding other lease options? Wouldn't this be a way to satisfy your needs of today while building on a bigger and brighter future?"

Well, that sounded almost too good to be true but I guess it could work out not to mention that if I then sold the house I could make a profit on it as well. Pretty cool.

Passageways to Riches #15
FSBO's

"FSBO's are a term in real estate jargon meaning, For Sale By Owner. Certain situations create a need for an owner to sell a property without the help of a realtor. More than often, the owner or seller is motivated to make a quick sale or they are trying not to pay a huge commission, which is around 7% of the sale price, to a realtor. On the sale of a $300,000.00

home, that is a commission of about $21,000.00, which is paid out of the sale price.

FSBO's are not always advertised by way of the media and they don't always have a sign in front of the property. When you happen to notice a house that appears as if no one has been maintaining it, or it may appear a bit run down like fences broken, newspapers never picked up, etc., these may be signs that it is vacant or the owner has had to leave suddenly. Jot down those addresses and find out who the owners are. All records are kept at the courthouse with that information. Sometimes you can go online to do this research. Remember, when you don't know, ask.

FSBO's are likely candidates for options and/or lease options. Get your birddogs to do some of this legwork, taking photographs of any likely prospects for you. Make sure to have the photos show the addresses when available.

Now, related to banks, money, retailing, wholesaling, and asking questions, I'm going to give you some homework assignments for tonight. Did you think this was going to be easy? Wrong, however it will get easier if you are having fun with it.

Assignment 1. Find this book and read it, 'Green Eggs and Ham', by Dr. Seuss

Assignment 2. Go out to dinner or breakfast and ask a decision maker, such as an owner or a manager, if they can do something a little extra for you. A little something above the norm. Make sure that you tell them how much you appreciated their service or empower them some other way so they can empower you.

Prizes will be handed out tomorrow. Be honest and fair. Most important, have a great evening and remember to:

FOCUS FOCUS FOCUS------I AM A MONEY MAGNET

Phew! what a long day. I felt pleased that the seminar was over, at least for the day. I wondered what Marlen meant by rewards? Probably some literature on his courses that I'm sure he's trying to sell.

As I was walking towards the doors to leave I remembered a thought that I had earlier. Our seminar room was like a ballroom. I imagined a seven-foot basketball player could not touch the head of the doors even if he was to jump and an entire herd of elephants could have entered thru all at one time. These doors were huge yet they now seemed small in comparison to the amount of people that had to clear the room. I noticed Melky waiting to speak with Marlen near the doors. There was a long line of people in front of him. Feeling sorry for him, knowing that it would take forever for Melky to talk with Marlen, I asked him if he would like to walk with us. Just that second Marlen announced that he was leaving and had to make a previous engagement. He said that he would see us all tomorrow and that we could ask our questions to any of the staff or speak to him at tomorrow's workshop. All of a sudden it was now referred to as a workshop. Melky smiled and said he would be honored to walk with us. I was now even more sympathetic to his slow hobbling with his cane. Rabbi Fred and I crept along with Melky out the doors.

"How would you like to go to Sabbath services with us tonight?" I asked.

"Thank you, but I live in a Chassidic community and if I was to go to Synagogue, it would be in my own community."

"Well, we're going to a very mystical and musical Synagogue and the music and services are awe inspiring. You could meet some really cool people."

Melky rapidly shook his head side to side and hobbled along. When we got to the hotel exit, Melky smiled with intensity, shook Rabbi Fred's hand, and started to say what I certainly felt was a very sensuous goodbye to me. He asked if we were coming tomorrow, on the Sabbath. I told him that I was coming and Fred could not. Melky then abruptly said he will see me tomorrow and hobbled away. His departure was both mystical and magical. He wore pastel colored clothing. As dull as the colors were, he had a glow like an aura around him. It was very strange. I couldn't put my finger on it but I knew in my own way, I was interested. How could he refuse an offer to be with me? Probably a good thing. I anticipated running into many men tonight that I was sure, would not reject me. I remembered that Rabbi Joseph Ben Aryeh was going to be a guest this evening. He is a renowned scholar and is known for his compositions on ancient homiletics. He has also written interpretations on Kabala and other mystical works.

I dreaded having to go back to Anna's house where I was staying, while in town. It was nice of them to have me but they had a full house of people from all over the place this weekend. Unfortunately, they were all women. Well, I only had to get dressed for the Sabbath there and hop a subway train back to Manhattan. Anna owned a cute little house but I certainly would not have chosen Queens for a place to buy. I must hurry. Shabbos is coming in around seven o'clock. No one is using the shower so I'll take advantage. Her shower is wonderful. All of these shower heads and all in the right locations.

It was getting late and I still had to light a yahrtzeit candle to commemorate the anniversary of my mother's passing one year ago. When I did it, I stood frozen with several memories of Mom. One of the last things she spoke to me about was to show patience. According to her, this would be the virtue I needed to find my soul-mate.

CHAPTER 4

A VERY TALL ORDER

I happened to remember a saying that Rabbi Fred used today. It was, "A man thinks and G-D laughs."

How true. It was already 6:15 P.M. and I now had to take a cab to the city since I had no time to take the subway. I flagged down a cab in Queens and wound up with a cabby wearing a turban on his head. I asked him how much it would cost to get to uptown Manhattan and he said thirty dollars. That prompted me to try one of those homework assignments that we got from Marlen. I thanked him for pulling over to pick me up and told him he seemed like a very nice man. I then asked him if he could take me to 75th street on the west end for twenty-five dollars. He actually said okay. When we got to the synagogue, as I was paying him he told me that I would have a very enlightening evening and weekend, then he drove off. Where did that come from?

I was so pleased that I knew almost everyone there. Some of them I had not seen in a very long time. There were also some Rabbi Aryeh groupies there to hear him speak. Bella asked me if I would like to join her and some friends for the Sabbath meal. Bella is a real piece of work.

People tell me that she sort of looks like me. She is a horny toad that wants everyone else's man. Since I was spending the night with her anyhow, I accepted her invitation. Soon after Rabbi Cohen spoke, he handed over the podium to Rabbi Aryeh.

Rabbi Joseph Ben Aryeh began to speak on the subject of Kabala. That was only the tip of the iceberg. The Kabala, he informed us, is composed of many different books and with a variety of subject matters within them. He explained the main topics of Kabala are letters, words, and names. When he mentioned names, I couldn't help thinking of Melky, actually it was the name Melchitzadek that I pondered. One of the main points he made was the Kabala teaches us different techniques on how to heal each other. There are apparently code words that when uttered and meditated upon, miraculous healings occur. After the service was over Bella had mentioned that Rabbi Aryeh was going to join us for Kiddush dinner at her apartment.

Rabbi Aryeh made the Kiddush blessings at Bella's for everyone. He gave us special personal blessings as well. He gave me a blessing that I should meet my Beshert soon and I should be able to recognize him when I do. After his blessing, I immediately asked him about the name, Melchitzadek. He explained the literal meaning of the name was righteous king. This referred to the king of Salem. Salem was a peaceful kingdom and Melchitzadek was a priest to the G-D most high. He added that this name is also believed to be another name for Shem, one of the sons of Noah and the predecessor of the Semitic tribes. Other descendants were Eber, whose name means to cross over. His passage taken was the crossing over the Jordan River. This is where the name Hebrew comes from. Another descendant was Abraham. Rabbi Aryeh then explained,

"Melchitzadek gave Abraham a special blessing. This was prior to Abraham being given another letter in his name, changing it from Avram to Avraham or Abraham. The letter added is inclusive within the holy Tetragrammaton name of the Lord. This, written in the book of Genesis and the portion of the Pentateuch titled, 'Go Forth,' or go away from your land. G-D speaks to Abraham and tells him that all the families of the Earth will be blessed through him. In the book of Genesis, it is mentioned that Abraham had many sons. We only know of Isaac, Ishmael, Zimram, Yakshan, Medan, Midian, Yishbak, and Shuach. There are several legends speaking about tribal descendants of Abraham leading all the way to Southeastern Asia."

Everything he discussed previously I had learned before but now he was treading on unfamiliar territory for me.

He said that the Cossacks were tribes that were descendants and followers of Genghis Khan. Then he said that the name Cossack had an etymology stemming from the Hebrew word, chazak, which means strength. He also shocked me with the fact that the name Khan is related to the Hebrew word kohain, meaning priest.

"There are other related priestly names like; Kahuna, the Hawaiian spiritual leader, Manto Khan, also called Manitokhan, the Native American tribal spiritual leader."

When I started ruminating on what he was saying, he then totally blew my mind.

"The Cossacks lived on the steppes of Southeastern Asia. On these plains, they learned to fight with the sword and were expert equestrians. They became famous guardsmen and point men in battle. However, they were ruthless and were often known to kill each other. They survived for centuries by pillaging villages and cities. He said there is a legend telling, from the strong, ruthless, and murderous Cossacks, that a slow evolution of their descendants will provide a righteous descendant. He will have certain powers that even he is unaware. He will perform miracles, only related to peace. When he will perform a seventh miracle of peace, this will merit the coming of the Messiah. The Rabbi then began to laugh and said we all need to perform random acts of peace, kindness, and goodwill, which is what will certainly merit the arrival of the Messiah and it should be right now as I speak."

"Amen!" the nosy busybodies answered.

I asked the Rabbi, with a smile and a smirk on my face, how real or true this seemingly esoteric legend could possibly be. With his left eyebrow raised, he answered,

"Esther Malka, Unfortunately I cannot quote my source, but many stories have been passed on for many millennia and for many reasons, by word of mouth. Even many of our laws have been passed on by word of mouth. Much of what has been written has been destroyed by those fearing sacred writings and by those who would not allow us to accept what is not so easily understood, or beyond nature and logic. The majority of those include the Greeks, the Romans, and others. You must understand that we live in a world that the Kabala refers to as the 'Olam Ha Sheker', or the world of falsehood. It is a world governed by laws of nature. Truth is constant and never changes. In this world, the only thing constant is change. Laws of nature did not totally apply during the times of the Temple. That was exemplified by the Ark of the Covenant, which had dimensions of length and width but did not diminish the interior dimensions of the Inner Sanctuary where it was used. The room had dimensions that did not change whether you totaled its measurements before or after the Ark was placed inside. This defied a law of nature that says all matter has weight and occupies space. When the Temple stood, G-D was nature and beyond nature. When the Messiah arrives, he will build the Third Temple in the place that Jacob recognized and called it Beth-El or House of G-D, which was also beyond nature. When all of us return to this House, we will be living in the 'Olam Ha Emet,' the world of truth. For now, in this world of falsehood, we must doubt the obvious and be open to what seems ridiculous or even beyond belief. There is an applicable famous phrase saying it may be wise to believe nothing of what you hear and only half of what you see."

He then looked at me carefully with a serious stare and said,

"When you said the name Melchitzadek, it triggered a memory of a legend that I hadn't visited since I was a child. The name was carried on to a future point in time. Another era and others called Melchitzadek."

I could tell that Bella was perturbed by the Rabbi's unfamiliar stories. She was always jealous of men because she wanted to be an orthodox Rabbi herself. She kept bouncing around as he spoke and then she sarcastically commented after he left,

"Some people are really electrifying; they light up a room when they leave it."

The next morning I had to hasten to sneak out of Bella's apartment. I arrived at the hotel at 7:30 A.M. This time I had my coffee, I ate, and I had more coffee. I consumed so much caffeine I became a total zombie. Melky suddenly arrived and bumped into me. I asked him how his evening went and he hesitated with a long pause. He then told me he didn't sleep very well but he had that grin on his face. He followed with the same question, and I answered that it was a beautiful and enlightening Sabbath evening. Melky joined me at the table where I was sitting. I asked him if he would like a cup of coffee. He said he had some on the way in and was good to go. In a sarcastic way I asked,

"What if I buy, my liege?"

He acted as though he didn't hear me and then stood up telling me he'll see me upstairs. He was almost too humble and seemingly altruistic. I appreciated those qualities yet I didn't fully respect them. I did know I wanted more attention from him. I actually craved it.

The room was much abuzz when Melky and I entered. At nine A.M. sharp, Marlen walked in and he was grinning from ear to ear. He asked the room to silence themselves and then began to call on people to share their experiences regarding our homework assignments.

The first man that was called on, George, said he walked to the library and found the Dr. Seuss book. He said he read it while at the library. He gave us a short report saying that it was a lesson in persistence. The book was a lesson that persistence pays off. Marlen said that was exactly right and he gave George a fifty-dollar bill. I was very P-O'd at myself for not having done the very same thing. Of course, I realize that you can't be in two places at the same time. That was my justification.

The next person called on was a woman named Susan. She said she went to a pizza joint for dinner and asked if they could do something a little extra for her. They told her that it was late and they were closing soon but they had plenty of pizza left. They gave her two extra pies to take home. Marlen gave her a fifty-dollar bill also. Everyone applauded and at least ten more hands went up.

Another woman, Bonnie, said she went to dinner with her husband and with another couple to a restaurant/bar. She said her husband complimented the waitress to the maître for great service. She then asked if there was a little extra something that they could do for the table. The waitress brought them three rounds of complimentary drinks. Bonnie said they probably would have given them more if they had stayed later. Marlen gave Bonnie another fifty and said that these rewards are only symbolic.

Next, some young man, Steven, said he went to some dinner club and wound up chatting at the bar with a man that turned out to be the owner. The club featured fine foods and live music. He told the owner that the band was great and he really liked the establishment. He said the owner gave him free drinks for the rest of the evening and offered him a job managing the club. He had never been there before and met the owner for the first time. He took the job!

Marlen immediately said,

"Watch your language Steven. Using the term j.o.b. is inappropriate speech in this seminar environment. I'm just kidding of course. We are not trying to tell you to quit your jobs. We are just trying to train you to think outside the box. I happen to know a lot of people that still have jobs but also make a lot of money with investments in real estate and other businesses."

Marlen took a vote on who should get the grand prize. Steven got the most votes. Marlen then gave him five, one hundred dollar bills. I'll bet he was a shill. He was only about twenty years old but he must have been working for these people. Marlen moved right along saying we had much ground to cover in very little time.

Passageways to Riches # 16
Cash Flow.

"People, all of us have needs to satisfy now, today. Building wealth generally takes time and some degree of patience. Doing deals like lease options helps to show positive cash flow however small that amount might be. If you compound that small positive cash flow and do it over and over again, you not only may satisfy those current needs but could build an empire! Keep your day job though. Never test the depth of a river by putting both feet into it.

Whenever payments received are greater than payments you have to make, then you establish a positive cash flow. This is also done when you have a deed and have to make payments in a buy and hold scenario, which we'll discuss later. If you are buying and holding a property and your payments are greater than the payments that you are receiving, then you have a negative cash flow. This is actually a common scenario for an investor that is trying to develop equity, but we are not teaching that here. It would only be a matter of time before your empire would collapse if you are doing that and on more than one property at a time.

I noticed Melky taking notes. I was getting a little bored. I kept thinking about last night. I slept at Bella's, and by myself. What am I doing here? I felt very lonesome. I started to look around but whenever I turned around to look, I could only find Melky. What is wrong with me?

I was getting drowsy so I laid my head over my arms leaning on the table. As I closed my eyes, Marlen's voice started to resonate in slow motion. I vividly remember him saying the word car. I felt myself driving a new car, maybe it was a Cadillac but surely a luxury car. It drove very smooth. On both sides of the road, all I could see were trees. They were all tall and about the same in height. When I looked straight ahead the perspective of the trees formed a V shape. I was at the mouth of the open V and the tops of the trees met at the base. Above the base were cotton ball clouds. They appeared to be red and orange. The sky was beautiful and bright. The trees were a shade of emerald that was blinding. I was driving fast, very fast. All of a sudden, even though it was daytime, the sky got darker and darker until I had to turn on my headlights. I became frightened and slowed down. Far ahead, at the point of the V, I could see a glimmer of light but it was so dark I could hardly drive. I was very scared because I had no idea what I was doing there or where I was going. In an instant, it began to hail. The balls of the hail hit the car hard making loud noises and it cracked the windshield. The balls were the size of baseballs. Then the hail stopped and the light transformed to brightness. It was like I drove through a light bulb. I was blinded and then I could see the most beautiful countryside I had ever witnessed. There was Kelly green grass that looked like fur. The trees were shaped as though they were smiling. There were patches of red dirt, dark red dirt, and all kinds of animals playing in the dirt. I was shocked and surprised as I saw wild animals playing with domestic animals. I saw lions and tigers cuddling with sheep and deer. There was some sort of familiarity about this scene and its timing. When I thought about the concept of time, I woke up to Marlen selling with his convincing voice,

"There are so many facets of real estate and every facet is a potential cash cow. There are sub categories to each one of these facets and what can help you most is to find a mentor, someone who knows the ropes. Someone that can spot the pitfalls if there are any and believe me I have surreptitiously found many. I cannot begin to tell you how much easier it is when you have someone taking you by the hand throughout the entire process. It is the safest way to enter a new realm. At break, go talk to some of our staff of instructors at the rear of the room. Go ahead and I'll see you in thirty minutes."

SEE YOU AFTER THE 30 MINUTE BREAK

I wanted someone to take me by the hand at this moment. I was awake but sort of in a daze. Everyone began leaving their seats at the same time and the crowd was moving very slow. As I got up from my seat, I met a woman who was strikingly gorgeous. She was sitting next to us and was totally enthralled at what Marlen had to say all morning. Whenever he said anything, she would sigh. I thought she was near orgasm a few times throughout Marlen's commentaries.

As the two of us crawled towards the doors going down the aisle, Melky was walking by. He stopped to ask what we thought so far. He quickly glanced at the woman's name-tag and said,

"Hello Anne." She answered in a bubbly manner,

"I can't believe how informative this has been. I have been a real estate sales agent for five years and I learned more at this seminar so far than I have since I began selling real estate."

"Gag me with a spoon," I was thinking.

Melky replied that he had heard many of these concepts explained previously.

"I thought I saw you taking a bunch of notes," I sarcastically disputed. He said that he kept having revelations that he thought he would just jot down. I asked if he and Anne could share what they covered today with me. Before they could answer, I asked Melky what revelations he experienced this morning. Anne immediately suggested that we go for coffee. Melky and I decided to go with her. When I repeated my question to Melky about what his revelations were, he answered,

"I felt very humbled. Becoming rich has nothing to do with who we are, but who we think we are. There are many rich people and some are fools. What separates them from us is the fact they are thinking it is okay to be rich. If I feel that I may not be deserving of riches, then I probably will create barriers, or impenetrable obstacles. Those will separate me from the attainment of wealth. But, if it is okay for me to become rich, at least in my mind, what is to stop me? Another revelation I had was that I think I am a really good guy. I would do many good things if I did have the means. I would love to give to charities and help those in need. I would also like to help many friends of mine that are in need. Therefore, why not be entitled to the means?"

Anne began to think that Melky probably was a person with good intentions, however, she said,

"Good people are not always rewarded well."

Melky immediately countered,

"It is true that bad things can happen to good people. I feel that if you set goals and follow through with them, rewards do follow. It all depends on what you think of yourself. If you feel undeserving, your actions will follow suit but if you feel deserving and act accordingly, the results can prove to be positive. It can be painful to accept the fact that we have everything that we want. The problem for many of us is that we don't separate the concept of wanting to want, and wanting something and doing what it takes to go out and get it."

Anne looked interested but she said she'll catch up with us later. She then marched to the back of the room and waited to meet some of the staff. We also proceeded to the back of the room but we continued on, out the doors. Melky was somehow walking almost effortlessly now and without his cane. He held the cane but was not dependent upon it. I asked Melky where he would like to go.

"I'll spring for breakfast," he said.

We walked to a tiny little coffee shop in the hotel. When we sat down he looked me dead in the eyes and asked me,

"What do you truly want from your soul mate, your beshert?"

I looked up towards the ceiling for some reason and answered,

"I want him to want to hear what I have to say. He will be interested in me. After much time spent together, he should still take notice of me and not take me for granted. I will know him and his deepest darkest secrets. I will accept him for who he is and cherish the time I'm with him."

It was as though Melky extracted these noble ideas right out from my inner-self that I have ignored since I can't even remember. Tilting his head to the side, he smiled and stared at me. I was agog and tried to stare back. How was he empowered to pull such visceral ideals right out of me? He then asked what I would like to order. I told him that I just gave him a tall order. He laughed and said he'll see what he can do. We ate and joked a bit. I began feeling a closer connection with him. Assuming that he was kind of broke yesterday, I asked him if I could pay.

"Absolutely not, I fell upon good fortune last night and thank G-D, I can pay for our breakfast. Not much else right now, but certainly our breakfast and I am honored to be in your presence."

He was certainly a gentleman. We finished and returned to the seminar.

CHAPTER 5

THE ORIGIN OF SPECIES

We approached the doors and I noticed the crowd at the rear of the room had grown considerably. Many people were being sucked in to inquire about the various programs Gandalph Enterprises had to offer. They must have charged good money for them. The truth is I felt a little less cynical for some reason. I thought that if these people can afford to spend their money on some real estate software, and / or other seminars, why not, enjoy! It didn't mean that I had to tag along with them. It seemed my mind was beginning to open a little. I became far more interested in what now appeared as propitious advice. Marlen was beginning to make good sense, at least to me.

Melky and I found seats next to each other in the center row and about the middle of the room. It was very noisy and many people had smiles on their faces. It was apparent they wanted more information, tricks, contacts, and maybe some magical channel to lead them to riches. I too wanted more and I think I wanted more of Melky as well. In general, his look was handsome. His face was kind of beaming while his head was covered by a cabby cap. He appeared warm and actually had a kind of glow to him. His hair had shiny grey wings under his cap. As I was assessing his overall look, he looked back at me. He had a smile as though he knew I was checking him out. I smiled back and wondered if he was interested, in me.

Passageways to Riches # 17
Buying and Holding

"Folks, when you are buying and holding, your goals should be that you are seeking a positive cash flow and/ or building equity for the purpose of selling at a later date for a larger profit. As in most cases, you must not fall in love with a particular house or property. Stay focused and leave your emotions at home, the home where you live. You must determine the value of this income property by doing a true assessment of its value. Use only common sense and inspect the property carefully. We use a checklist that is offered along with many different contracts that you can use, some for buying and different ones for selling. All are legal of course. You need to properly determine the value and not base it just on an appraisal from a professional. You have to be that professional! You should also figure out what the net potential income will be. Remember you are trying to build a steady stream of income. To determine the cash flow you should use costs and annual property operating data. Here again you want to purchase below market value, figure any renovating costs, and everything else until you can establish your net profit and or your positive monthly and annual cash flow. You want to know your ROI or your return on investment.

When you have bought houses you created debt. Your goal is to pay that off from your newly found income from the property. To maintain a positive cash flow, your rent must be charged at a greater rate than your payments, which will reduce the amortization or the principal amount of the loan with some of it going toward the interest on the loan. This process will increase your equity on the property.

This form of real estate called buying and holding does take time and often years to build up the equity. If you maintain that positive cash flow, then one month at a time you will accumulate wealth and seemingly out of thin air. Cumulative effects are another subject that we'll discuss a little later in the seminar."

Marlen asked if anyone had any questions. While some people were called on, I started to strum up conversation with Melky regarding tonight's concert at the House of Loving Prayer. While I was yakking, I noticed what looked like a priest asking a question to Marlen. He was sitting in the second row from the front of the room. I wanted to hear so I put my finger to my mouth when Melky was answering some stupid question I asked about the seminar. He shut up and I caught Marlen asking the person if he was a man of the cloth. The man replied,

"Yes, I am a Priest."

He obviously was since he was wearing all black with a short white collar protruding his lack of a jacket collar. He questioned Marlen,

"What if someone had invested in say ten or more homes and then the recession got so bad or a depression broke out to the point that all of these homes had lost their value? How would you feel if you were mentoring someone like that and they were on their way to the poor house?"

Marlen began to clap his hands and then half the room started clapping.

'What's to clap about,' I thought.

"Forgive me," Marlen said, "but before I answer your question I would like to tell you a short story that you reminded me of. Is that okay?" he asked.

The priest began to smile which was a 180-degree turn from the expression he had on his face when he asked Marlen the question. He nodded to Marlen and Marlen proceeded

"There was this Professor of Microbiology and Bio Chemistry. He happened to be an agnostic."

Everyone started laughing and Marlen went on with his story,

"The scientist approached a Priest with a problem and asked,

"Father, please help me. I have a son who has been groomed to be a doctor or a scientist like myself. He has been given a very costly and good education. He has had Professors that are far greater than I am. My son has often been disrespectful of them and is no different at home. He answers me back with nasty adjectives and is intolerably unkind to his loving mother. Where have I gone wrong?"

The Priest hesitated for a moment and then replied,

"The difference between us is that you have been taught the Darwinian theory of evolution, the origin of species that Man has evolved from the ape. The religious mindset is that we believe man descended from Adam, the first man who was created in the image of G-D. The biblical characters mentioned in the Bible were mostly righteous men and women. Even the ancient sages were great. As time has passed, we have devolved to a far lesser than righteous mankind, subject to far more and heinous sins. For us, much respect is given to our fathers and forefathers. To your son, he feels loftier than his monkeylike forefathers and ancestors, so it seems natural for him to think less of his elders."

When the priest who asked Marlen the original question shook his head in agreement, Marlen continued,

"The priest admitted to the professor that he believed in Angels. He said,

"The virtue of Angels is that they cannot deteriorate. Their flaw is that they cannot improve. The flaw of Man is that he does deteriorate; but his virtue is that he can improve."

Marlen smiled and said he loves that story. Some of the people applauded. He then went on with an answer to the priest's question,

"When we are mentoring we literally take our students by the hand with a step by step method which can lead to great success. These methods are proven. Each and every one of our mentors has a proven track record of success. It is also true that anyone who has tasted and experienced success has also had failures. The recipient of failure can succumb to failure or pick himself back up and re-group. Now, we do not encourage anyone to put all of their eggs into one basket. When you are buying 10 houses and you are using our practice of buying far below market value, then you have a deal. There are many ways of finding these good deals and we will hopefully have time at this seminar to discuss some of them. Everyone needs a roof over his head. Yes, it is also true there is a down market right now in Real Estate, however, this is a time to buy very low, and during times of a recession, the Real Estate market actually goes through inflation.

The United States are on sale right now. You can buy houses for pennies on the dollar and there are many motivated sellers. This is a marvelous time to buy and we teach how to buy right. One of the challenges is the money. We use Other People's Money. If they cannot afford it, they will not let us use it, but it is there or elsewhere. We never put a lot of money down, if any at all. We also teach the goals of win-win systems. The last things I can tell you are we have a large database of good people who need a house, a home, and we want to help them find one.

Thank you Father that was a real good question. Now let's move on.

Passageways to Riches #18
Selecting Contractors

Are there any contractors in the room?"

About 10 hands raised.

"That's not uncommon to see at these seminars. There is of course a common synergistic interest between wealth, real estate, and construction. You contractors may not like what I have to say about this profession but if you think about it, you may agree.

Well, here it is, you see, contractors are like dolphins. Dolphins have been known to bring happiness, joy, love, and creativity to the oceans. That said, there have been studies done in San Diego, California involving many dolphins. As they were taught to do tricks, like jumping through hoops, their patterns were observed. In the beginning, they were rewarded with fish to eat when they would successfully jump through a hoop. A pattern eventually developed which showed that after a while they knew they would be rewarded with a fish. Soon they realized that all they would have to do is barely clear the hoop and they would still be rewarded. Sometimes all they did was swim around in a circle, acting as if they were trying, expecting a fish as a reward. This is parallel to something called Theory X management. Its premise is that work is inherently distasteful and avoided whenever possible. Offering more fish or more money to do the tasks at hand will not necessarily be a solution. You will merely be giving a greater reward for a diminishing work output.

I hate to say it but there are times when certain contractors can be compared to alligators. Alligators generally fear humans. Tourists that don't know any better will feed the alligators, which in turn convert the vicious animal's fear into perceiving humans as easy prey.

Getting back to dolphins, the dolphins understood what was expected of them and they complied, anticipating a reward. Much the same, a contractor will initially try to show you what he is capable of and will want to secure a position with you. He will put in the necessary time and effort, sometimes even more. After a while though, if the efforts appear to diminish, remember the dolphin theory. New contractors should be sought out whenever this pattern is revealed. You should all familiarize yourselves to the time and costs of doing various types of construction work. Am I right you contractors out there?"

A few smiles were tacked on to these contractors faces and no answer was given as though they were guilty and in agreement with Marlen.

"That is all I am going to say about contractors right now because we have to move on. There is a lot more to be learned about the selection of contractors, which our courses also provide. Let's move on to:

Passageways to Riches #19
Hiring Advisors

People, all of your friends will give you advice. Anyone that you talk to will provide you with advice. The problem is that very few are qualified to give you good advice. You want to build a team. Business and investing is a team sport. You want to deal with experts, using their expertise, speaking their lingo. You need these foot soldiers out there to make sure things are happening correctly. By building a professional team, you will save time and money. There is no I in Team. If you are the smartest member of your team then you're in trouble. You are, however, the leader and you're searching for leadership. You want to teach your advisors the three mandates of leadership:

1. See things as they are but not worse than they are.
2. See things better than they are.
3. Make it that way.

Your advisors are leaders themselves. Stay clear of followers. Those are like sheep. A flock of sheep may hang together well but their only accomplishment is to eat grass. When delegating, describe the outcome of what you want. Ask them what they need in order to get the end result you expect. Agree on a deadline with them and then, follow up.

You may be looking for a Professional Realtor, a Mortgage Broker, a Lawyer, or Lawyers, all of which happen to be specialized professions. Be careful in your selection for a lawyer in particular. How do you know when a lawyer is telling a lie? His lips are moving! Just kidding. There are many lawyer jokes but don't let the joke be at your expense. Lawyers are attorneys. The word attorney has an interesting etymology. It is derived from the Latin, atorn, meaning to turn over. Some have the ability to take the truth and turn it over into a lie and vice-versa.

Before you turn over all of your money and your businesses, make sure they are on your side."

I couldn't help but think to myself, Marlen said he was an attorney. I wondered who was turning over for him.

"But people, lawyers, not liars, are professionals that you must deal with. You must develop a relationship with them. Sometimes they don't know what it is that you are trying to do and you must be able to explain. I have had real estate attorneys argue with me about land trusts, shelters, taxes, and other things. If and when that happens, get a second opinion. Sometimes it's best to pattern yourself after a Missouri mule, also known as a Jack Ass, who stubbornly allows his will to dominate his choices and not allowing the influences of others. Don't be discouraged. Get your deals done in an optimal legal fashion. Lawyers are people and people can make mistakes. Just keep the mistakes to a bare minimum.

You will also often need a Contractor that is also a specialized professional. You will need a property inspector and evaluator, a Property Manager, a CPA, etc. You will delegate assignments to these foot soldiers so your time will be spent doing the more important things like finding more deals. You should find birddogs, who will assist you also in finding qualifying prospects. The best way to find these people is to get references from independent and impartial sources. Don't use people involved in your transactions because they could prove to have a conflict of interest. Find people with good reputations with people you trust. Don't hire the bottom of the barrel just because you are new to the game. Be confident and talk to these professionals. Explain what you are doing and tell them what it is that you expect them to do for you, not how to do what they do. Be honest and don't accept anything but honesty in return. Keep in mind that although you have your team, they represent you and you could be liable for anything that they do. No matter what it is that they are doing, you will want to double check them. Never criticize, chastise, or complain about your staff. Stimulate and motivate them.

If you can't manage your own money, you may not have any to manage! You don't want to be like a lemming who follows the others to their potential doom. Just watch where you are going.

Our courses provide you with a perfected checklist and a long database of professionals to assist you with experts in all of the related fields. Reward those that help you. Team is an acrostic for **T**ogether **E**veryone **A**ccomplishes **M**ore. If you have 24 people working for you an hour a day, you're working 24 hours a day! Think outside the box.

Okay everyone, it's 12:30 now. We'll see you in one hour and fifteen minutes. That's 1:45, don't be late. Go ahead and talk to some of the staff during the break. Pick their brains and have a good lunch."

The room was so crowded with people standing that Melky and I decided to wait until it became manageable to walk out. We stayed in our seats and started talking about the material just covered. Melky spoke in a somewhat deep voice but very soft spoken and gentle. I was hypnotized by his cadence and tone. He was asking me a question, which I seemed to have missed, so I quickly changed the subject and asked him if he wanted to go to lunch with me at a synagogue nearby. He said that would be fine and I told him where it was that I had in mind. The synagogue was only three blocks away.

As the room was clearing, we approached the doors. Melky, while passing a woman in the aisle, accidentally knocked her notebook out from under her arms. He immediately bent over to pick it up and simultaneously she did the same. Their heads collided when they began ascending. Melky had her notes then in hand and while returning them he apologized. While handing back her notes I noticed him reading the nametag on her blouse just adjacent to her cleavage. Her name was Lucinda. With a pompous alacrity, she told him to call her Lucy. Of course, she was compelled to ask him if he was enjoying the seminar. He answered that he was indeed interested in all of these concepts being presented. I then interrupted asking her if she was learning anything here and before she could answer, I introduced myself since Melky didn't have the presence to do so. In a bubbly, affable, and high-pitched tone of voice, Lucy looked me right in the eye and answered that she was tickled pink to be here. She went on to say this seminar had presented her some golden opportunities. Curiously, I asked her what she meant. In so many words, she told us that she was an investor with a deep pocket that she acquired from an inheritance. She told us that she met a few people here that already had some potential deals requiring an elephant. I didn't understand the jargon but judging by her figure, I knew that she didn't mean she was a fatty. She was in fact very well built and quite voluptuous. Her breasts were popping out of the low cut blouse she was wearing and didn't seem to mind flaunting her physical inheritance. Another older woman had caught up to Lucy in the aisle and informed her that she now had the paperwork for the deal they were discussing earlier. Melky and I gave our salutations to the bubbly booby woman and proceeded to the rear doors.

It was already twelve forty-five by the time we got to the doors and our lunch break was diminishing. I was getting hungry and urged Melky to speed it up a bit. He agreed and informed me that he too was hungry and looking forward to a Sabbath meal. We passed through the hotel room doors and caught an elevator car as soon as we got there. Down we went with smiles on our faces.

CHAPTER 6

ABRA C' DABRA

As Melky and I descended to the ground floor in this glass walled elevator car, we couldn't help but notice a commotion outside of the hotel exterior doors. With my usual feline curiosity, I hastened to the front of the hotel doors on Broadway, which happens to be a brilliant location for this huge hotel on a street dedicated to all of the tourists and locals of New York City. Melky was several steps behind me when I opened the door and some guy was pushed right into me. He almost knocked me down and Melky dashed out to grab my arm. As I regained my composure I realized that there was a fight ensuing. The fight involved two men, one a black man, and the other an Arabic looking man wearing one of those shawls with tassels at the fringes wrapped around his head. It was the Arab who was pushed and he began to retaliate. Melky stepped in front of me to address these apparent adversaries. Surprisingly, Melky then shouted out in a loud tone of voice that even caused me to back up a few steps. The two men froze in their tracks and Melky quickly asked what was going on.

I now had to look over Melky's shoulder to see exactly what was going on. Both men and even a bystander all started to answer at once. There were probably around ten people surrounding us. The pretty woman that we met at the last break, Anne, was also now standing next to me. It was still chaotic until Melky raised both of his hands upwards perpendicular to his shoulders with his elbows pointing outwards. He then softly uttered the words,

"Abra c'dabra".

I was stunned and felt a cold shiver in my bones. There was immediate effete silence. In an orderly fashion the Arab spoke first saying the black man tried to rob him. After that sentence, Melky then turned to the black man who said that the Arab took money out of his charity box, which he was using to collect the money for a local charity. Then the bystander said he himself had it all wrong, assuming the Arab was joining with the black man to steal the $500.00 that the bystander happened to be counting at the time. Out of the clear blue sky, the two, actually three adversaries shook hands and apologized to each other. The Arab explained that he put a $5.00 bill in the box thinking it was a $1.00 bill. When he noticed it was a five-dollar bill, he tried to exchange it for a one-dollar bill. When the black man assumed he was trying to steal some of the cash from the box, he tried to protect it. The black man finally understood and said it was very generous of the Arab to give him the dollar.

Before the black man had left this scene, Melky told the bystander who appeared shaken, that it would probably bring him great fortune on this occasion to put 10% of his $500 in the charity box, if he could afford it. Without hesitation the man pulled out a $50.00 bill and put it in the black man's' box. I seriously wanted to escape this surreal scene and suggested to Melky that we leave for the synagogue. The Arab was still present and overheard me. He looked at Melky and having overheard me, he said,

"You're a Jew aren't you?"

Melky turned around to face him.

"Yes, I am."

The Arab began to comment,

"I have lived in this city for ten years. I am also a descendant of Ibrahim who you know as Abraham. I, on the other hand, have Ishmael as an ancestor, and you, his brother Isaac. You displayed much courage to involve yourself in this altercation. I have never experienced an outsider to embrace danger in such a manner, particularly in this city. When you raised your hands I almost bowed down to you and I have no idea what gave me such a feeling other than thinking it was Muhammad himself appearing, and came to defend me. I would like to thank you and bless you with success."

I was now so stunned I froze but as Melky took my hand I felt warmth and comfort. Melky then bowed his head a little toward the Arab saying that his charitable act will also grant him success and fortune. Melky then bade him a farewell. As if there wasn't enough confusing dialogue at this point, Melky told the Arab to wait a minute. He let go of my hand and put his hand on the Arabs back. In a quiet voice he said,

"Our people are all Shemim, Semites, who are descendants of Shem, one of the son's of Noah. Our families have fought long and hard enough. Our true martyrs are those deceased and the living that have been touched by the hands of destruction who have watched their loved ones perish. When they decide to forgive and yet not necessarily forget, when that happens, which it will, this World will become Paradise. Salam, Habibi."

The Arab looked awed, and then replied,

"Shalom, Habibi."

Melky walked over to this stone frozen creature, yours truly, and again took my hand. When he took it, I melted and the crowd dispersed. I knew I was walking but the kinesthetic connection between my mind and body wasn't there. It was as if my feet were jelly. I looked up at him and noticed a glow on his face. Right at that time his hand began to burn mine. I let go and he apologized as if he knew what was happening. It was all too much for me to inquire about this anomaly but I did ask him about the words he used when he raised his hands. He asked that I please wait until we get to the synagogue. I accepted his request and we walked toward the synagogue. As I walked, I kept replaying the entire experience, over, and over, in my head. There was so much going on that I just couldn't fathom.

We finally got to the Synagogue and there was a large group of people already eating the Sabbath lunch. It was a buffet style with a beautiful array of fish including herring, salmon, whitefish, and sable. There were also multiple salads. I was pleased that we were early since the meat dishes were not out yet. Orthodox Jews don't have fish on the table while they are serving any meat dishes. We found a table and sat down. Melky began reciting the blessings on the wine, chanting a beautiful melody that I had never heard before, and then we washed our hands in the traditional fashion before eating bread. Melky then made the blessing for bread and we started eating.

Just as I was about to ask Melky to satisfy the slew of questions I had, an older woman walked up to Melky and recognized him. She started talking to him informing Melky that his Grandfather used to study scripture with her father who was the Chief Rabbi of Chicago Ill. The woman was very well dressed and looked good for an older woman. I was hoping she would hurry up and leave us when she then coerced Melky to meet her family. I was pissed when Melky obliged her and left the table. In a matter of minutes, they served the meat platters, which were a spread of cold cuts and chicken. I dug in and before taking my first bite, some nice looking man walked up to the table asking me my name. I was happy that we left our nametags back at the seminar. I told him my name and he introduced himself as Brian Greene. He asked me if I came to this synagogue often and I said no. I told him I usually went to the West side and prayed at the synagogue called The House of Loving Prayer. He knew where that was and said he would be going there this evening after the Sabbath. I remembered there would be a concert this evening and told Brian I was also going.

It was getting close to 1:30 and I told Melky that we had to get out of here. When I spotted him engaged in a conversation with the Rabbi, I again noticed something strange. Brian was now sitting next to me and I asked him to look at Melky. When he looked, I asked him if he noticed anything out of the ordinary.

"Not really, but he has a nice tan or sunburn."

That didn't add up, I thought to myself. He had an aura around him and it looked like some other people noticed it as well because many were staring at him. I rushed Melky to join me in after blessings and we left. On the way out, I told Brian that we would see him tonight. I was now in a state of desperation to understand all that had transpired earlier, after we left the hotel. I stopped Melky as soon as we got outside. I wasn't sure where to begin but I asked him,

"Melky, when you uttered abracadabra, was it a perfunctory command or was there a meaning for it?"

He explained,

"Abracadabra is a form of Hebrew acronym. One of its meanings is that I will create like a word. Bora is the second word in the Bible meaning create. Dibur means word or can mean thing. The k sound in between the two words is a prefix, meaning like, or when. There are four ways to study the Bible in its original language known as the Holy Tongue. They are:

The simple literal translation,
The allusions,
The homiletic interpretations,
and the secret hidden meanings.

Much is lost and misconstrued when only the simple translation is used. The first sentence of the Bible is, 'Breishit bora Elokim, ait ha shamayim v'ait ha aretz.' The simple translation is, In the beginning G-D created the heavens and the earth.' The letters or alphabet used in the origin of the Bible, called Aleph Bet, has for its second letter a

Bet and even sounds like a B. You see, the first four words are Breishit bora Elokim ait…The word ait is technically a part of speech known as the particle of the accusative that presents the object in all of its phases which represents all of its characteristics. That's a lot for just a two letter word. Not only that but the word ait, has no meaning. There are no ineffectual words just thrown into the Bible without meaning. Ait is spelled Aleph Tav. They are the first and last letters of the Aleph-Bet. This demonstrates that in the beginning, G-D created the A to Z, or the letters he used to utter the words, which indeed created the Universe. According to Jewish and Christian Kabala, it is believed this happened several thousand years before the creation of the heavens and the earth. When the Aleph was used before the bora to create the word abra, the Aleph, which is silent, originally took place in the realm of chaos and it was a void. When I said abracadabra, I created a void for myself to understand everything that was happening, and allowed the men to experience that void to gather their thoughts. Somehow, it worked for us."

"Wow," a prolific and complicated explanation satisfied one question I had, but it also birthed new and more questions. I then asked him why he thought they were eager to put money in the man's box. He answered,

"These men somehow recognized that it was a vessel for charity. It isn't always, but this black man was collecting for an entire neighborhood of poverty-stricken people. Charity is a form of using currency for its proper intent. Currency means to flow. In addition, the gift of charity is one that always flows back to you. There are levels of giving charity, like you should not infer that the recipient is less than you, for you might eventually be the recipient from the same person or group. To give without expectation or just for the sake of giving is very high level and happens to pay great dividends."

When we got back to the hotel, we went back upstairs and the doors were already shut. Melky seemed a bit upset because we were a little late. The doors weren't locked so we entered and Marlen was speaking. I had to sit in the rear of the room near the seminar staff. They were busy with their computers and some were listening to Marlen speak. Melky went up one of the aisles and disappeared.

CHAPTER 7

DEATH AND TAXES

Passageways to Riches #20

Setting-Up A Business

"Yes everyone, this is our next subject. To do this you will need to provide for yourself, tax shelters and a good Certified Public Accountant. Look at the projection screen and it will show you where you can hold your wealth building assets.

SOLE PROPRIETOR
LIMITED PARTNERSHIP
PARTNERSHIP
ONE MEMBER LIMITED LIABILITY COMPANY LLC-1
MULTI-MEMBER LIMITED LIABILITY COMPANY LLC
S-CORPORATION
C-CORPORATION.

If you are in the pursuit of a profit, the IRS considers you to be in business. A Sole Proprietor is where one person receives all the profits. This type of business is taxed at your personal income tax rate. If your business has no potential for liability and you have no other employees, then this could work for you. Here, everything you own is at risk. There are basically two types of partnerships: One being a general partnership, and the other being limited. A Limited Partnership can shelter its partners from personal liability exposure. It has at least one general partner and one limited partner. A general partner in either case has full liability. A limited partner only has liability to the extent of his investment. A One Member Limited Liability Company can shelter its owner or owners who are called members, from personal liability exposure. Interesting that in a Multi Member LLC, the profits are not necessarily divied up proportionately. It also will be taxed as a partnership and not as a sole proprietorship.

An S Corporation is taxed like a Sole Proprietorship or a partnership. It can shelter its owners from personal liability exposure. There are restrictions to the number of shareholders and types of shareholders allowed. This type of corporation can be excellent if you don't expect to earn much money. It is good for a service corporation relatively new and that may start off losing money until it gets on its feet.

A C Corporation pays its own taxes at the current rate of about 15%. Advantage could be taken of the graduated tax tables available to the corporations and their employees. There are a great many more benefits for a C Corporation but a well thought out plan, should be made first. Obviously a good accountant or better yet a CPA is necessary to the team for deciding which type of business category suits you best."

Passageways to Riches. #21
It's None Of My Business

When Marlen read what was on the projection screen I looked around to see if I could find Melky. I didn't see him but I noticed some of the people here fell asleep. I felt like doing the same especially after the corporate stuff. People going into business to lose money and all that, yuk!

"Selecting a business to own requires some thought. Are you personally capable of hiring or even firing employees for that matter? Are you a leader? Do you have a budget? And, can you sustain yourself and or your family without a paycheck? Before you venture into a successful business, make sure you can satisfy the needs of today. If you currently have a J.O.B., you can invest in or create a business part time. Do you have a plan? Is it long term or short term? When you have these answers, then you can proceed. You see, businesses are usually for the purpose of making money. The health of a business is measured by the income and the profits that it generates. It can be fun to be in control and it could be terrifying as well. A business leader and owner must be prepared for all possible outcomes.

A business does not have to be started by you. It is possible to purchase a business or even trade for one. If the business is your idea, you will want to protect and secure it. If it involves a product, you can buy and sell the product in either wholesale or retail. If it is a service, you might be able to sell it after building a database of repeat clientele. You can do all this and more all through one particular business.

To be successful in your business, you should be unique in your particular niche. People want to be recognized and on a personal level. It is key to establish personal relationships with those that you even speak to. That one item can generate a greater longevity. Create a brand that people recognize when they see it. Make them want your brand. There is no greater PR than word of mouth. Good news travels quickly but, so does bad news.

During the Reagan years, I was doing construction work as a Foreman carpenter through the Carpenters Union. The rules had then changed regarding a ratio of one apprentice allowed for every seven journeymen, to one apprentice allowed for every three journeymen. Obviously, the quality control went down the toilet since the labor for apprentices was so much cheaper than journeymen, they were the popular choice. As a carpenter foreman, I was liable for everyone that worked under me. If someone from my crew would have been killed working on the job, I could have been liable for manslaughter. For that responsibility, I was paid an extra dollar an hour. When they cheated me out of that dollar, along with the fact that I had four apprentices working for me that were all an accident looking for a place to happen, I quit!

I wound up going fishing for the next two months, which pretty well exhausted my savings. It was time to get a J.O.B., so I looked in the newspaper and answered an ad to be a car salesman. To be a car salesman in the state of California I had to get a special license from the state that cost me $50.00. The dealership where I went to work had a very lazy sales manager. No one in the whole place was willing to teach me how to sell cars. What their intentions were for me was to be a 'liner.' That is the meeter-greeter who turns over the potential buyers to a salesman that closes the deals. I decided that I would learn how to open and close my own deals so I could make the entire 25% commission on the gross profit for the dealership. I went to the library and found a book written by the greatest car salesman in history. You see folks, if you want to earn more you have to learn more. The product knowledge about the cars I learned from the manufacturer's brochures. The greatest auto and truck salesperson in history was none other than Joe Girard. He is now a motivational speaker teaching seminars. What I learned from him was persistence, follow up, and giving customers great deals. It was paying off. People gave referrals and I would have repeat clientele 3 or 4 years down the road when the Average car buyer trades in on a new vehicle.

I began turning into a car-selling monster. I was as strong as an ant that humbly bores tunnels carrying great loads on his back and at a rapid pace. I was salesman of the month every month thereafter. They had a plaque on the wall for that title and they kept changing my name from Marlen Gandalph, to Marlen Whiteshoes Gandalph, to Whiteshoes Gandalph, etc. It was embarrassing for the other salespeople there. Then they decided to fire me for prostituting their merchandise. Even though I was awarded a bronze medallion from Chrysler Corporation for selling over one hundred units in six months, I was selling too cheap! I was shocked that a retail business like this would have management too lazy to sell a lot of product. I was into volume sales anticipating future clientele. That was the secret to longevity in this competitive business.

Well folks, the good news is that here I am now. I just sold three car dealerships that I owned and turned all of those formerly losing propositions into profitable businesses. I used the same techniques that I learned from Joe Girard. As I said, you can develop a business and sell it for a profit whenever you want."

I began getting a little bored listening to Marlen's story and then shifted my thoughts toward the dream I had yesterday. I was wondering if Melky would be able to help me understand the meaning of my dream. I started dozing off again. I began another dream. This time I pictured myself with a house and I had three male roommates that were my tenants. The three of them were paying me what totaled out to be more than the payments, which I had to make. I had bought a four-bedroom rancher with two and a half baths. It was located in the borough of Queens NY and was very pretty. When it was time for me to collect rent from the tenants, one of them could not pay me. They each had their own bedroom and the guy that couldn't pay me had the largest bedroom in the house. He wasn't very attractive but he was kind and considerate. He asked if I could wait several weeks, which was when he would be receiving a large inheritance.

He said that when he received it, he could help me by investing enough money to help pay off the house. I was forced to say it would be okay. At that point, he kissed me. The kiss was friendly at first and then became quite romantic and sensual. We wound up in my bedroom and one thing led to another. In the morning, I woke up and he was lying there next to me, sound asleep but with a smile on his face. I made some coffee in our huge kitchen and as soon as I took a sip, I woke up to hear Marlen,

Passageways to Riches #22
Commercial Real Estate

"Please understand everyone; doing commercial deals is really similar to doing residential deals. You are still looking for motivated sellers. The basics are the same but watch this,

> apartment buildings,
> office buildings,
> strip malls,
> industrial properties,
> storage-centers,
> mobile home land,
> retail stores,

and there are more that compile an area called commercial real estate. One of the beauties is the fact that they have a tremendous potential for larger amounts of income and monetary appreciation. They present the potential for larger amounts of cash flow. You want to determine the amount of cash flow and that will dictate the size of the properties you want to focus on.

For example, if it's $15,000 to $20,000 per year, and you are looking into apartment buildings, you will need to find 10 to 15 units. A multi- unit apartment residence can potentially replace your j.o.b. If you are currently earning 25 to 50 thousand per year, you will need at least 20 apartment units. If you are earning 60 to 100 thousand dollars per year, you will need 50 units plus.

Continue doing your single-family residences and build your real estate portfolio. Remember the only difference between 100,000 and 1,000,000 is zero so don't be afraid.

If you have lots of income and you need another tax shelter, this market becomes very intriguing. You should also be aware to protect your credit and pay back all loans. This issue is very important in commercial real estate.

Besides the real estate associations, it would behoove you to join apartment associations and attend their meetings for finding real estate prospects, banks to deal with, and potential partners for larger deals. If you have become proficient at managing properties, you may find partners like doctors and lawyers who do not have the time or the expertise to do it themselves.

Hey folks, you know the song, 'We gotta move on.'

Passageways to Riches #23
Property Management

I couldn't manage to take my attention off Marlen's apparel. He was certainly cocky and a bit arrogant but even that didn't coincide with today's outfit.

"My friends, not only can we spend little time on this subject here and now, but a lot of time can be wasted on the very management of properties as well. Your goal should be to delegate a large portion of managing your properties to others so you will have more time for priorities, which is another subject matter we will discuss further on in this seminar.

Here is how I select my tenants. I first have a generic questionnaire which all tenant prospects must fill out. When they come to me or to one of my property managers, we look at their teeth. Yes, you heard it right we look at their teeth. We are not dentists but the way they take care of their teeth can reveal the way that they take care of themselves and how they will take care of my properties.

When they arrive at my property or my office, I also make it a point to take a glance at what they are driving and I do so discreetly. What do they have on their floorboards or in the back seat? Better yet, what does their trunk look like? If it is a total mess or trashed out, I wouldn't be surprised to find the very same with my property in the near future.

It takes a special demeanor to be a landlord. You must not be a softy yet you should have understanding compassion. Having management companies and realtors on my payroll know this and they are familiar with my policies and procedures. Their primary job, besides collecting the rents, is to help me qualify the tenants and follow up on potential problems. Again, having a management team buys me time.

Passageways to Riches #24
Buying Notes and Liens

Guess what everyone; we are not teaching you to write or even purchase love notes. In addition, 'laying the note' is certainly not something we would teach, since it is illegal to shortchange people. I had to learn about that while doing a hostage negotiation in a men's prison."

Thinking of love notes made me want to pass one to Melky. I don't know why, but I already miss being near him. I still couldn't find him. Funny, I felt like I was being held hostage away from him.

"Well, this subject is often referred to as the paper business. No, not newspapers, toilet paper, paper cups or paper plates. These are personally held mortgages, trust deeds, and government sold liens. All of which can be secured by real estate property in the event of a default.

You can buy partial or entire personally held mortgages and often at a discount. Those that hold such paper often need cash now and cannot wait for monthly payments even with all of the interest accumulated. It is possible for example to buy a $100,000 mortgage for say $75,000. If you bought such a mortgage, you would generally be entitled to the monthly payments and in the event of delinquency, you can foreclose and take over the property.

A safer and far less problematic paper to invest in are government liens. Most often, when owners default on tax payments, liens are attached to their properties. Until these payments are satisfied, the property cannot legally be sold. As a buyer of these liens, you pay the delinquent taxes and then you take over the legal position of the county or state.

The yield from the payments can be much higher than you would receive if you deposited your money into a bank. Of course, that would constitute the most liquid place for your money but your investment in a lien is secured by the real estate. If the owners make the defaulted payments you are guaranteed government legislated returns of 12% to as much as 36% in interest, depending on what State you are in. The rate of return is fixed by law. You also have the potential to obtain these properties for pennies on the dollar.

Get this; personal credit to purchase liens is not an issue. Purchasing deeds and liens can be well suited for retirement plans.

Passageways to Riches #25
Taxes and Insurance

Folks, you are probably wondering how taxes and insurance can be a passageway to riches. This topic deals with the structuring of purchases and sales. Here however are the last two subjects of what is called PT and I. Principal, Taxes, and Insurance. Obviously, these cost you money and there is no way around taxes and insurance. They say there are two things that are for sure, Death and Taxes. Frankly, I am not too well informed about death. You would have to consult Mr. Joe Black on that subject but, the penalties for not paying taxes can result in financial penalties, foreclosures, and time spent in the property belonging to the government known as the Grey Bar Hotel.

Minimizing and or eliminating expenses can lead you on the passageways to riches. Spending money needlessly is wasteful, sinful, and pitiful. For example, when you sell a property and you show a profit, it is called a capital gain. There are ways to avoid paying large capital gains taxes, like filing 1031 tax-deferred exchanges on like kind properties. Like kind properties are defined differently depending in what state of the nation they are located. These specialties of taxes and insurance are best handled by conferring with your CPA and your Lawyer.

When I was 11 years old, I had a j.o.b. working for my uncle during summer vacation from elementary school. He was a television repairman. One of his customers was the daughter of the famous actor and comedian, Eddie Cantor. We had to go to her apartment one day to check out her tubes. No, not those tubes. In those days, televisions had tubes, which would burn out and need replacement instead of the tiny transistors and conductors on printed circuitry that we now have called solid-state circuitry. Well when we got there, she was crying. When my uncle tried to console her, she explained that she had to give up her standard sized poodle. A standard sized poodle is the largest size poodle there is. The name on the poodle's collar was Bambi Cantor. Bambi was huge.

My uncle told her that he had a wonderful home to take her to, which happened to be my home. She was sad to relinquish the dog but happy that she found a wonderful home for her. My father taught Bambi many tricks and gave her commands in any of 14 languages that he spoke. Okay folks, this story is slightly related to our next subject,

Passageways to Riches # 26
Stocks and Bonds

In 1929, Eddie Cantor became a very disgruntled Goldman Sachs Trading Company investor. According to him,

"They told me to buy the stock for my old age… It worked perfectly. Within six months I felt like a very old man."

The GSTC stocks went from $326.00 a share to $1.75 a share in 1929. That was the beginning of the great depression. If he had held on to that long-term stock, he would have come out of it eventually with a profit.

Frankly the types of stock that I prefer are physical. Something that I can see or hold in my hand. That said, there is money to be made and actually, stocks have proven to be the overall most profitable investment over the last fifty years. The best stocks are long term and they need to be held, even through recessions. If you cannot afford the luxury to hold them that long, then perhaps you should stay clear.

Important to know that the brokers who sell the stocks get paid to play with OPM. Play, because the stocks may or may not make any money. They charge a fee to set up an account and if the stock loses, the broker still gets paid.

The optimal way to make money with stocks is to sell your own. You can do that if you incorporate selling to shareholders and that way you will be on the inside and in control.

Our team of advisors have very modern computer software that can help you if you have the desire to invest in stocks. Never put all of your eggs in one basket.

Well, that ends our day with the passageways. Listen everyone; please have your thinking caps on tomorrow because we still have a lot in store for you along with some surprises. Get some rest tonight and we'll see you tomorrow."

Everyone applauded and proceeded to leave. I found Melky and now had a moment to ask him to join me tonight in attending the concert at the synagogue on the west side. He said that he wanted to take the evening to ruminate on the last two days but then suggested that we stop for a light meal first. I thought, why not. This would provide me the time to ask him some other unanswered questions.

I noticed on my way out that people were already writing checks to the staff at the rear of the room. We kept on going and rode the glass elevator down. It was already dark outside. I looked at my watch and was surprised that it was now 7:30, much later than I expected. We walked uptown a few blocks and found a cute kosher restaurant that was open. Melky told the maître d that we would like to sit upstairs. I found the atmosphere a bit romantic. Melky ordered a rack of lamb dinner so I followed suit and ordered the rib steak dinner. We were attentive to our surroundings and both of us acknowledged that it was indeed a nice cozy atmosphere. When the waiter brought our salads, I asked Melky if he knew how to interpret dreams. He said he knew a little bit about the Jungian methods and studied dream interpretation after a series of vivid dreams that he had personally, previously encountered. I first told him about my dream driving along the highway.

While waiting for an interpretation, I dressed my salad with oil and vinegar. He asked me what this dream meant to me. I tried to understand and then just responded,

"If I knew that, I wouldn't have asked you."

"Easy Esther, I can help you try to understand its meaning and I believe in this case that there is an important meaning. I don't want to dress your dream with false interjections. A dreamer is the one who often gets a message through a dream. The connection inevitably winds up with the dreamer. I do think I understand a part of the message but I want you to strive to make the connection."

"Please just explain it to me."

He asked me what a luxury car meant to me. I answered,

"It feels smooth and glides along the highway where you can go fast and not feel the road, or the speed."

Just then, the waiter returned to the table with more bread and asked if we would like any more salad. We thanked him and told him we're good.

Melky was quick and a bit pertinacious to imply,

"Your dream has a simple and yet a complex understanding. We are on the brink of the coming of the Messiah. It may be his first, second, or who knows how many comings. We can see that the world is in a present state of chaotic behavior, meaning the weather, the corruption, the wars, etc. This is what has been prophesized. You were both a passenger and a driver to experience a transition, which finally led to the realm of the lion dwelling with the sheep. You also had a ride that was bumpy symbolized by the hailstorm and battered windshield, but it was smooth enough for you to steer through it. That means as the driver, you had to do something yourself to help bring the Messiah, be it perhaps, random acts of kindness or love of your fellow man."

As I thought about what he was saying, I sensed that his interpretation was accurate and Rabbi Aryeh said the same thing about the random acts of kindness. The waiter then brought our main course.

"So what is it that I have to do exactly?" I asked,

Melky laughed saying,

"We all want to know what to do for this to take place but the answer for you personally is something I can't answer. You have to figure it out."

I then I told Melky about my other daydream earlier this afternoon. I began to take a bite after cutting off a small forkful of my steak. Melky again and now in a somewhat pretentious manner asked me,

"What does living in a house with three men mean to you?"

"Well, I used to live in a house with three brothers."

He then asked me if I loved one of them more than I loved the others.

"I suppose I love my youngest brother the most. I was the oldest and after my mother died, last year, I had to take the role of mother with him."

He asked if I might understand any other meaning to the dream. He said that a dream can only most accurately be analyzed by the person who has or had the dream. I thought about that for a minute and pictured Melky in the role of the tenant that I slept with. I answered Melky,

"There are three men in my life that I would like to live with and maybe have a serious relationship with. I know that I am monogamous and could only be with one."

I wondered if he figured out that he was one of those three men. With a cocky facial expression he began to answer with a lower tone of voice.

"Esther Malka, you are an attractive young woman. You are younger than I am and your desires that pertain to a soul mate are going through a state of transition. The tenant that you slept with represents a male with qualities and requirements much like your youngest brother. You want to be needed and wanted like all of us. He has the potential and promise to bring happiness into your life."

I felt like he was reading my mind and quickly glanced at my watch. I told Melky I needed to hurry so I could be at Bella's apartment, get dressed, and then get a ride to the concert at the synagogue. He smiled and I sensed he wanted to come with me. I asked him again if he wanted to come but he said he had to tie up some loose ends, whatever that meant. We finished eating and Melky left a generous tip. He also paid for my dinner. I flagged down a cab while he waited with me. When the cab arrived, he gave me a gentle kiss goodbye. I felt the kiss all the way to Bella's.

CHAPTER 8

THE WISDOM OF AN APACHE INDIAN CHIEF

On the way back to Bella's apartment I also kept wondering what chances I had to win Melky over. I didn't know why I was having any doubts. He complimented me, telling me I was beautiful. Why was I so attracted to someone that was at least ten, maybe fifteen years older than I was? There certainly was a mystique about him. In the past, I have always been confident about my ability to attract anyone at will. Hell, I'm a magnet, but whom have I been attracting? Idiots like Richard and nerds like Fred. I want Melky. He's older but he's easy to look at and smart in a humble fashion, not to mention, magical. He also seems emotional and that could be a good thing. He apparently knows a lot about the lucrative business of real estate. Maybe he will soon get rich and comfort me with necessities of life.

I was able to hitch a ride with Fred going to the concert at the House of Loving Prayer. It was only a short ride uptown and he wanted to discuss the seminar with me. He had all kinds of questions about today's seminar. I told him we were on # 26 in the top 50 hit list of the Passageways to

Riches. He said I shouldn't be so damn cynical. He never once asked about Melky and that was a good thing since I wouldn't have known where to begin. I told Fred that I would rewrite my notes so he could read them after the seminar was over, possibly tomorrow night. We made plans to leave for the seminar at 8:00 A.M. tomorrow morning. We arrived at the House of Loving Prayer just in time for the concert to begin.

Surprisingly, my focus was on the music instead of all the men that were there. The place was packed. The musicians were all playing instruments I had never seen before. There were two stringed instruments. One resembled a lyre. Then there was a funny shaped woodwind, and a box that a woman was beating on with rhythms in an unusual time signature. I learned to play piano when I was young and could still play but I never heard such foreign rhythms as these. The harmonies were at times dissonant but always returned to sweet mixtures that were quite pleasing to the ear. They only played one long set. Afterwards Rabbi Cohen gave his little speech about special events coming soon and then closed with a prayer and a blessing for us all.

Brian Greene showed up and spotted me talking to Bella. His approach was suave and I could tell that Bella had the hots for him. Watching her gloat over him was typical of her and disgusting. She invited him to her apartment and told us that Rabbi Aryeh was going to be there again. I found that interesting but at the time, I was happier to find Brian's attention was mainly on me and not on Bella. He was rather well dressed and quite well mannered. I put on my best face so he would stay focused on me. Bella had a small apartment which was now full of people. Brian sat next to me and asked me who this Rabbi Aryeh was. I told him that he was a popular Kabalist that liked to mingle with younger people. Rabbi Aryeh once told me that he was able to draw liveliness from younger people's uninhibited strengths. I felt proud that the Rabbi spoke to me on a first name basis. While we were schmoozing, Rabbi Aryeh joined Brian and me. He told me that he had other thoughts related to what we were speaking about the other evening. I became most curious and asked

Brian if he would excuse me for a while. Brian politely headed toward the pastries that Bella had put on the table. I then confronted Rabbi Aryeh face-to-face while Bella was all over Brian. Rabbi Aryeh said,

"Last night, as I was saying my blessings before retiring, I kept thinking about Melchitzadek. For someone of such high stature, his mention in our scripture is minimal. Of course, where we find Melchitzadek is in the Chumash, which in the language of the Holy Tongue, literally means five. Chumash Chomshei means the five books of Moses. While I was focused on that, it reminded me of the Chumash Indians from the coastal areas of California. The Chumash tribe is actually pronounced, shoomash. The first Chumash people lived on Santa Cruz Island. It is told that after the great flood, from seeds of a magic plant they were created and by the Earth Goddess, Hutash. She was married to Sky Snake, who we call the Milky Way. With his tongue, he made lightning bolts that once started a fire. This is how the Chumash kept warm and cooked their food. As the Chumash grew in numbers, Santa Cruz Island became too populated and the noise of the people annoyed Hutash. She finally decided to make a bridge to the mainland out of a rainbow, which connected Santa Cruz Island all the way to the mountains of Carpinteria on the mainland. Hutash convinced the people to cross the bridge but a few children looked way down to the water, got scared, and fell. Hutash felt guilty for convincing them to cross and turned the children into dolphins. To this day the Chumash feel like brothers to the dolphins."

When Rabbi Aryeh mentioned dolphins, I started to think about Marlen's analogy of contractors, working in construction like Melky. Rabbi Aryeh had more to say about the Indians.

"I then remembered another legend. It was a legend that had a very special meaning and a strong connection to me. During the times of the early settlers in Western America, a Native American tribe of Apache had a medicine man that had most unusual powers. His own people were fearful of him but they were not afraid to disagree with his desire and focus on other options for peaceful solutions when battles were ready to commence. This same medicine man was responsible for creating an environment where he taught squaws and children how to read and write. This was unheard of at that time. Some of the tribesmen called it the devil's work. His goal was to educate them in literacy so they could teach others. Very few men could read and even fewer could write.

One of his disciples was a young boy. At the age of five, the boy began learning from this shaman medicine man. The boy was actually destined and groomed to become a chief of this Apache tribe. He learned many secrets from the medicine man and among them was the ability to make peace. Amongst the various tribes, there were often battles for food and territory. Then, besides the tribal wars, there were wars with the Mexicans and with American settlers. As the boy grew older and witnessed many of these battles, he learned the attributes of becoming an Indian chief. He had to learn to be eloquent, generous, impartial, industrious, and contentious. When he turned thirteen years old, he was tested in all of the Apache dietary laws. There were after all, forbidden foods like the bear and the snake, etc.

Once during a performance of the Sunrise Dance, which is the ceremony for girls entering puberty, his tribe was attacked. The chief of the tribe was murdered and many warriors were killed. The remaining adult men that survived summoned a meeting after the battle and decided that this boy was the wisest choice to become the new chief. Miraculously, no longer considered a boy, and now the new chief, he moved the location further west for his tribe and for the next ten years the tribe grew while living in peace.

Also moving west, were the settlers who randomly began attacking his tribe. The tribe had well trained warriors that knew how to fight guerilla style, managing to prevail in many of those attacks.

One day his people were doing their usual chores and a handful of American soldiers randomly decided to attack his village. There was no apparent reason for the attack. The well-trained warriors from his tribe were actually victorious. The warriors took a white soldier captive from the battle and it so happened to be a general from the Union Army. The general, after defeat, was humiliated and yet embarrassed by the actions of both himself and his unit of men. He lost almost all of the men in that unit and began to feel guilty for the unprovoked attack. He was taken before the entire tribe for them to decide how they were going to kill him. The general was tied to a tree and many of the tribesmen suggested torturous and horrible ways to kill him. An argument arose and the chief stood and raised both of his hands. All became silent and squatted to hear the chief speak. He spoke in the Mescalero tongue, which was the language of his tribe and accurately translated everything into English for the general to understand. He told them all that it is time for the killing to stop. He said that one of the precepts for an Apache was to live and let live. Of course, when under attack, they must defend themselves and protect each other's lives. He went on and on about the beauty and value of life. He described a vision he had regarding the white man moving west and populating the lands of the Apache in great numbers. The chief then spoke about learning to live with these white strangers and what would happen if they did not, alluding to becoming extinct. He then gave a dissertation about man.

"Whether white or Indian, every man has a shining hour and a time of significance. The moment might only be brief. A man may also have his foolish moments. He may commit sins."

He explained that a sin in the Apache tongue had the same meaning as an archer missing his target or being off the mark and then he explained the correction.

"When you are far from your target, you must aim high or higher. You might see a man lose himself and do something absurd. Do not judge him in haste. Every human being is vulnerable to a moment of weakness, despair, or pettiness. This man may have had domestic stress, a failure in his way of hunting, or doing his business and perhaps it depressed him to the point of action beyond reason. Remember the man will have his fine moments too. Be generous in your judgment, considerate and compassionate in your conclusions. The memories of our past have colored our minds, but keep in mind it is only a reflection. From sympathy comes fondness; attachment; love; infatuation; devotion; rapture; adoration; and perhaps even to being smitten, as I am by my squaw.

The apparent boundless contradiction between tension and ease creates motion. An arrow in flight is in a different state of rest at any given moment and at that time, it is not moving at all. Yet, when it strikes the buffalo, it becomes obvious that the arrow moved swiftly enough to bring down the large beast. Without such apparent contradiction, there would be no movement, and hence, no life. Change is all that is predictable and change is what we are to experience, particularly now and forever. What was once hot will become cold and what was once wet, will eventually dry. We must never feel too secure with our habitat, because hunting, governments, education, and businesses, are as subject to change as man himself. That is truth in nature. It is only the divine will of Wakan Tanka, the Supreme Spirit that never changes."

He asked that the warriors untie the general and called for a special prayer meeting in his tipi. They followed his order and he invited the general. First, most of the men were to take a ritual steam bath.

Does that sound familiar Esther?"

I kind of nodded in affirmation, assuming he was referring to going to the Mikvah, our ritual bathhouse. That prompted me to sound a little insolent so I said,

"Oh yeah, like being baptized."

"Similar," Rabbi Aryeh said while smiling.

"When they entered the large tipi of the Chief, all of the men sat in a circle. The Chief carefully picked up a peace pipe sitting on a three-legged stand. He lit it up, and then he stood up, cautiously holding the bowl of the pipe with his right hand near his heart and the stem with his left. He raised the pipe up towards the sky. Then he lowered it down towards the earth. Then he pointed it in the other four directions while saying a short prayer,

"Wakan Tanka, Tunkashila, Onshimala…."

That translates to; Grandfather Spirit, pity me, so that my people may live.

He sat back down and drew on the pipe blowing the smoke out of his mouth and nose. Before he passed the pipe to his left, where the general sat, he explained that the smoke was symbolic of freedom like buffalo breathing on a cold day. When he passed the pipe, he explained it was a very special one. The red stone bowl came from a quarry, which were the remains of all flesh and bones turned to stone from the great flood that took all life in its time. He said that smoking the pipe was for Mitakuye Oyasin, meaning all of his relatives:

The inanimate,

The plants,

The animals,

The humans, we are all one universal family. He said more precisely, that it was for mankind, who is always capable of self-destructing.

He then told the general many of the qualities and useful things that his people were capable of performing. The Chief, although pessimistic in his outlook, grew optimistic in his preparation for the future of North America, just a microcosm of the spiritual Universe.

The general was awed over the wisdom of this chief. He himself had a vision in the tipi of how the white man and the Indian could live in peace. The next morning the warriors prepared a horse for the soldier on which to ride off. Before he left, he confronted the Chief. The general asked the Chief his name. He explained that a medicine man gave it to him when he was eight days old. It was the Mescalero equivalent to 'righteous chief.'

This very same Union Army general, years later, became instrumental in a treaty that left the Apache nation of the Southwest, an area of 16,000,000 acres of land in an area called Four Corners, bordering on 4 different western states."

Rabbi Aryeh then added that he has heard other legends of men having the same or similar names that represented a righteous king. He then explained that tzadikim or righteous men were rare and very few have been known throughout history. He said there was always at least one per generation that had powers strong enough to make a peace that could merit the coming of the Messiah. Again, the task was to bring more G-Dliness into this World to make a dwelling place for Him, Wakan Tanka if you like, yes, in this World."

I asked Rabbi Aryeh how he knew so much about Indians. He corrected me by replying,

"It would be politically correct to call us Native Americans. My Father is a Native American and my Mother, of blessed memory, was an American born Jew."

After I thanked Rabbi Aryeh for sharing his wild story with me, I began to wonder what Brian was doing and hoped he wasn't bored out of his mind. Other than the fact that Rabbi Aryeh was stressing the principles of making this a more peaceful and moral world in order to make a dwelling place for G-D, I thought it was a little unusual to reminisce on stories that didn't involve characters from our own liturgies. There certainly was no shortage of Jewish forefathers or sages for that matter. Why tell stories of Indians and Cossacks. It was however, interesting that he spoke of a boy being given a name at eight days old, similar perhaps to a Jewish Briss, when a boy is given a name and circumcised. Another subject of interest was mentioning the great flood and then moving that peace pipe in the six directions, similar to the ritual we do during Succos, the Festival of Booths, shaking the four species. I think the four species consist of a willow branch, myrtle, a citron, and a date palm. I'll have to ask Melky.

Relating his stories to Melchitzadek was very interesting and I suppose geared towards my initial question of who this Biblical character was, or is. Nevertheless, it started me thinking about Melky. I wondered what he was doing on this beautiful evening. He could have capped off the evening with romantic overtones that might have given me a perfect grand finale.

As Rabbi Aryeh said his goodbyes, Brian left the kitchen and Bella then asked me if I would like to get a cup of coffee somewhere else. Frankly, I was happy to leave the presence of this particular crowd of the pretentious and pompous friends of Bella, so I agreed to leave with him. When we got down to the front of Bella's apartment building, I told the doorman that I would return later. He smiled and said he would be there all night.

I was a bit surprised that Brian began to flag down a cab. I thought he drove here. He said he had a car but didn't use it when traveling around the city. He took me to some late night coffee house that was rather quiet and peaceful. I asked him what he did for a living.

"I'm a scriptwriter and a playwright."

When I told him I was an actress, he became surprised and somewhat elated. I asked him if I may have heard of anything he wrote. He said his most recent play was called,

'Return to Happiness'. He said it played only three weeks on Broadway. I asked him what else he had written and he said his penultimate play was

'The King and The Servant'. I quickly responded with,

"Are you kidding? You're Brian Greene?"

"I thought I introduced myself." With a chuckle he added,

"Aren't you, Esther Malka?"

"Yes, we just finished a two week performance of 'The King and The Servant' at the Newyorican playhouse on the Eastside. Esther Malka is my Hebrew name, my stage name is Queen Rose."

As Brian's forehead rolled and folded practically all the way down to his nose, he asked,

"You're Queenie?"

"That's me!"

"I didn't recognize you. I watched your first performance there. You all did a marvelous job of acting out my intentions."

I apologized for never having met him. He said his schedule has been hectic as of late and he was currently working on two other screenplays.

"Wow, that's a bit like multitasking, isn't it?"

He explained that he cheats.

"Many of my stories have a common theme."

He said that the only difference between 'The King and the Servant' and 'Return to Happiness', is that they take place about two centuries apart. Other than that, he said he loves writing these kinds of love stories. He added that he likes happy endings.

"If anyone ever asked me to do a different kind of ending, I would have to reject it. Happy endings are sort of my trademark."

I asked Brian why I didn't see him at the closing party after our last showing. He said he was in Los Angeles for a preview of the same play.

"Well, how was it in comparison to ours?"

I believe he was sincere when he said that he liked our cast better. His phone rang and I happened to look at my watch and saw it was already two in the morning. It sounded like he was talking to a woman. After his conversation I told him I better be getting back to Bella's apartment and he flagged us a cab once again. On the way back to Bella's he was quiet and I began replaying what had happened today in my mind, thinking about Melky.

When Brian dropped me off he offered to walk me in but I told him I was fine seeing the doorman right behind the doors. He did ask for my phone number and I gave him my cell phone number. He then gave me a peck on the cheek and we said goodbye. The doorman gave me a funny look like I had perhaps stayed out too late. I got into the elevator and had to wake up Bella to get into the apartment. I apologized while she just turned around and marched back to her bedroom. She did have the couch covered with a sheet, blanket, and pillow for me. I must have tossed and turned until five in the morning. At seven A.M. Bella was up and ready to go jogging. She asked if I wanted to join her. I tried to sound most regretful and explained I was running late. My idea of exercise is a night out clubbing and dancing. I left the apartment at eight and hustled to the other side of the city for the last day of the seminar.

CHAPTER 9

THOUGHT, SPEECH, AND ACTION

Fred picked me up at Bella's a little after eight. We had just enough time to grab a coffee at Starbucks. I got a large double espresso black. I needed a fix, I was so tired. I took my coffee to a seat near the aisle about four rows back and Fred strolled in right behind me. I thought I would save a seat for Melky. I turned around to take a tally of all who were still here. That wound up being just about everyone that had begun the seminar. Most everyone looked ready with their briefcases, notebooks, and pads of paper to collate more data, which they anticipated receiving today. Some had on their Sunday best but most were in their Sunday casuals. Fred was his usual disheveled self with wrinkled shirt and black pants, which were a little too short in pant length revealing all of his white socks above his shoes.

When Marlen galloped down the aisle I still could not find Melky, yet I sensed he was here. When Marlen screamed out,

"How is everyone?"

I nearly jumped out of my seat. Of course their reply was,

"Great"

It was as if I wasn't all here just yet. Marlen told us that this ship was about to sail and we better put on our life jackets. What finally woke me up was the suit that Marlen was wearing. It was purple with a red ascot draping out of his breast pocket and he had purple shoes to match the suit. Who did he think he was dealing with, the mob?

Marlen suddenly asked for a volunteer. I raised my hand up quickly. Marlen called out my name and I knew he could not have seen my nametag because it accidentally got turned around with my name facing my chest. I got excited when he asked that I please come to the front of the room and I ran up there. He had a large tablet of paper on an easel and handed me a marking pen. He then told me to draw a horizontal line across the center of the page.

"Okay Esther Malka, now think of a subject that you are very familiar with."

"Drama," I said.

Marlen instructed me to draw a vertical line upwards from the center of the horizontal line.

I drew the line and he said to write drama next to it. While I was writing <u>drama,</u> He asked me if I could possibly teach drama.

"Of course, teaching is another subject that I am familiar with."

He then told me to draw another vertical line going upwards and write<u> teaching.</u> While I was writing, he told everyone to draw the same kinds of lines and write what was appropriate for them.

"Okay now think of another subject that you know a lot about and write it on another vertical line."

I had to think for a moment but wrote <u>piano playing</u>.

He said to keep thinking of other subjects and write them down.

I then wrote; <u>Bible Study</u>; <u>Raising children</u>; <u>meditation</u>; <u>flower arranging</u>; <u>cooking</u>; and <u>dancing</u>.

Marlen asked me what kind of dancing and I answered,

"Ballroom; Modern; Ballet; Latin; and Cajun."

"Great, now add all of those to your list since each one is a specialized form of dancing.

Folks, the horizontal line you have drawn, represents your life. In your lifetime there is no doubt you have gained expertise in any of an infinite amount of experiences that you have had. Our next subject matter here is,

Passageways to Riches #27
Internet Marketing

Let's give a round of applause to Esther Malka for volunteering to share with us."

I went back to my seat but noticed Fred and Melky sitting in the front row saving me a seat. Before I sat down, I was hoping for a hundred dollar bill, which I didn't get, but it was pretty cool to get called on and I found this information rather interesting.

"Every single one of us has a niche or a specialty we enjoy doing and that can be a starting point in business. This is the information age and there are endless amounts of specialties that people will pay you to share and teach to them.

You will find that you have more than one, if not many specialties that you can market and sell to others. Think hard as you write these down and you will probably come up with many.

When you will learn how to set up blogs and web-sites, you will find that you can also be paid to advertise similar or related products belonging to others on your own sites. These are called affiliate sites. You can get paid per click, paid per reference, and/or paid per sale.

Our experts will teach you the most effective ways to set up these sites so you can be off and running in a very short amount of time. Speaking about time, these sites require very little time to manage once they are set up. Realize that there are hundreds of millions of people buying on the internet and this is a fantastic time to get involved in this business even if it is a supplemental business.

Ladies and gentlemen, our next four subjects are related to each other but each is a separate entity."

The projection screen lit up with;

Passageways to Riches #28
Communication

Passageways to Riches #29
Speech

Passageways to Riches #30
Semantics 101

Passageways to Riches #31
Negotiation

For a moment there, I thought this was going to turn into an English class. Marlen explained,

"Communication sounds like a simple and hackneyed subject matter. Surprisingly many of us fail to do it, or at least to do it properly. The definition of communicate is to share. It means to have a connection and it is a means to a bond with another or others. Sharing is a two-way street. The primary reason the divorce rate is so high is that one or both parties does not hear what that other party wants. Think about that. If your mate tells you that he or she wants pasta and you firmly believe that nothing could be more loving than to give your mate a chateaubriand steak, then you have not qualified that you are giving your mate what he or she wants. Essentially, they may feel that you are unwilling to make them happy. Happiness, to your mate, at least at that particular time, is having pasta!

To communicate with others you must establish a rapport. Since communication is a two way street, you have to be willing and be able to listen. Hear what they are saying. Hearing requires focus. Read their body language. In fact use all of your senses but do so in proportion. Remember you have 2 eyes, 2 nostrils, 2 ears, 2 hands, and 1 mouth. That is what we mean by, 'in proportion.' We actually teach communication using a science we call, 'Multi-level meta-linguistic comprehension'. It deals with observation, understanding body language, and speech inflection.

Let's look at this from the other perspective. In order to get what it is that you want from others, you must communicate with them in a way that they are inspired to want to give it to you. If this sounds banal or worse yet, manipulative, then you are overlooking the fact that communication is an art and should be cherished as such. Good communication can by itself, and resting on its own laurels, save a marriage and even give a greater longevity to a marriage.

We are all too often influenced by our own ideas, observations, and experiences. This can close our minds to the beauty of perhaps experiencing something new. If you can create an open minded, open-door policy to at least listen and possibly welcome suggestions and/or ideas from others, you can open the passageways to successful communication.

Dancing is a form of communication, isn't that right, Esther Malka?"

I was now quite attentive, however I almost missed the fact that he was referring to me, but when I did, I nodded in affirmation.

"Good dancers, particularly in couple dancing, circle dancing, and line dancing, have the practiced ability to mirror each other, meaning their steps are identical. In verbal communication, mirroring involves matching another's speed in speech, volume, tonality, and body language. In short, if someone is whispering to you, he or she will anticipate that you whisper back, etc. Watch and experience patterns in communication. When you introduce yourself to people by your first name, notice that they will do the same. If you use your first and last name, they too will use both. This is known as a comfort zone that you will create.

Beware of lazy communication. What I mean by that is do not make assumptions or use generalizations. Make sure you are understood to others as well as make sure you fully understand them.

When you assume you make an **Ass** out of **U** and **ME**. Analogies are okay but they need to be used at the right time. We will learn more about analogies later.

Most all of us can speak and there are many ways to speak. More than just by using your mouths can you convey thoughts. In my lifetime, I have had the pleasure to meet eloquent people that were mutes! People sometimes speak with their hands or facial expressions, just to name a few. That being said, I have also met blind people that could see clearer than most.

Public speaking is a form of communication. It is also one of the highest paid professions and has a cast of some very powerful people. How do I know this?"

When the seminar attendees started laughing, I found myself wanting to hear more. This was interesting and I thought it was applicable to something that I needed to learn.

"Isn't it strange that there is a statistic, public speaking is more feared than death by suicide? Speaking in front of others merely takes a bit of practice to be perfect. Look in the mirror and practice what it is that you have to say. When you are planning a speech, realize that you have only one chance to make a first impression. Be prepared.

We need to understand that all thoughts are part of the manifestation process. Thoughts are physical and even more so is speech. When thoughts are converted to speech, the only step left to create something is action. Speech is the powerful pre-requisite to action. If you use speech to tell people repeatedly of something you intend to do, it becomes more real. This can be a powerful tool for breaking bad habits. If you tell people that you are going to lose weight for example, your mind and physical actions will begin to act accordingly. We here at Gandalph Enterprises, call this process, 'Normal Psycho-Neural-Physiology.' We'll get into that a little later.

Semantics have a strong and profound effect on people. Most beliefs are nurtured by words. They can also be altered by words. Theologians have been known to take vows of silence. I'm not saying that you shouldn't speak but it is better to be silent than to say words that can be harmful to others. 'Sticks and stones can break your bones but words can shatter lives, if not destroy them. They can also empower lives with the select choice of words.

Do you remember this? 'In the beginning was the word and with the word, G-D created the Heavens, the Earth, and all creation.' What does that tell you?

You are what you think you are and what you say validates and creates your reality. Your past has probably been poisoned with negative metaphors, parables, and analogies that are limiting you in your quest for riches.

'Only the rich get richer,'

'It takes money to make money,

'Owning a business means being a workaholic.'

None of this is true unless you are programmed to believe it is true. Realize that nothing has any power except that which you give it.

'You're fat and ugly,'

'You'll never amount to anything.'

The list goes on and on. Do not believe in lies. Realize that you were created in the image of G-D. If you feel fat and ugly, don't eat so much and move more.

Be careful when you begin a sentence with, 'I am....' What you say, your mind and body will duplicate! Make positive statements.

'I am beautiful'

I am rich'

'I am a money magnet.' Of course, you want to believe what you say and you can if you are thankful or grateful for your current resources. Not until then can you have more.

Oxymoron's can have an effect as well, if you accept them:

Social Security;

Military Intelligence;

Jumbo Shrimp;

Federal Reserve;

Save Money, Buy Here;

Political science;

Petty cash;

Pay through the nose;

Environmental Protection Agency.

Outgrow your old baggage. Yesterday is a cancelled check, tomorrow is a promissory note. All there is is right now. A bird may fly over your head and land something on it, but you don't have to build a nest there. Do not become your own worst enemy.

There are a few common words that you should stay away from using, like, 'I'll try.' If you try to pick up the papers that are in front of you, they will not move. If you try to move, you will go nowhere. Trying indicates not doing. Trying is a lazy way out of doing. Do you remember the movie, 'Star Wars,' when the guru master Yoda told Luke Skywalker to levitate the spaceship? Luke's answer was, "Master, I'll try." Yoda reiterated with, "Try you mustn't, do you must."

Another word you should avoid is can't. Is it true that you won't or that you don't know how you can? Ask yourself when you are tempted to use this word, "How can I." These lazy words will weaken you and your goals.

How about the word impossible, There was a time when many thought it was impossible to fly. Impossible to send letters and pictures through phone lines. That one still blows my mind. Send letters or pictures across the world through cyberspace, Of course, it's impossible to fly to the moon. Run a three- minute mile. Ride a motorcycle over Snake Canyon. David to slay Goliath.

It says in the Bible that for G-D, nothing is impossible. Having been created in His image, we can emulate Him. Don't make excuses by using words or statements like:

I hope.
I should.
I would if I could.
Be true to yourselves and be true to others.

You also don't want to inhibit yourselves by making statements like

'I have a bad memory.'

You will tend to believe what you say. If your memory is bad and you continue to make that statement, your memory will get worse! Besides all that, there are methods and exercises that you can do to improve short-term and long-term memory loss. We happen to teach some of those methods.

Let's move on folks to negotiation. The optimal situation in a negotiation is win-win. I guess you know by now that I like to make analogies using animals. The dolphin, for example, loves to play win-win games. He will even generate eye contact with you while playing such games. He will also lose interest when playing win-lose games.

Rewards in negotiation will not always be in the form of money. You need to do your homework to anticipate what it is that they might want in exchange. Probe them, ask questions, and always watch for their response. The three E's in negotiation are:

Establish, Elaborate, and Emanate.

The good communicator can get someone to ask him what it is that he is selling, and believe that it was his own idea.

If you are negotiating to make a purchase, make it Subject to….

An inspection,
An attorney's approval,
A phase 1 or 2 environmental report, etc.

Keep the leveraging and negotiating points in your favor. Always have the end in sight. Know what the seller wants and needs. You can be willing to show him how it is that you arrived at the price or your offer. Be honest and show them comparable deals.

After you have completed a negotiation, make the other party feel good. This isn't a power trip. Tell them that they negotiated hard and won some points.

Well folks we're going to take a coffee break. I'll be in the back of the room with the staff if you have any questions so far."

I felt like I had tons of questions but I was beginning to recognize many of these topics were indeed passageways to riches. As the three of us left through the doors, Marlen was shaking hands and acknowledging people's names as they too left the room. As we passed Marlen, I could only focus on the stigma of the purple suit that he wore.

Leaving the hotel I had a chance, while out of earshot of Fred, to ask Melky a question.

"Do you have a girlfriend or significant other?"

"No, and if you don't have a husband or a jealous boyfriend in the Mafia or the Hell's Angels, I would like to take you out sometime."

"Does that mean you want to take me out on a date? I told you I wasn't married and I have no boyfriend, let alone a jealous one, period."

"Well, why don't I take you for coffee today?"

"Give me a rain-check and let's go for coffee anyway with Fred today."

Melky nodded affirmatively and we walked a little faster to catch up to the usual fast-paced Fred. He seemed to be leading us to a place he knew of. We wound up at a Deli about two blocks away. After we ordered, we sat down and Fred asked us what we thought about Marlen's dissertation on communication. Melky was the first to answer,

"The Kabala says that the three basic laws of manifestation are indeed: Thought, speech, and action, and in that order."

Fred agreed and while laughing, said that he thought Marlen might be a closet Jew. We all started laughing.

I asked the guys, "What was with Marlen's getup today?

Fred answered,

"Although it is a sin to cross-dress, the rich and famous basketball player, Dennis Rodman, used to dress like a bride with orange hair to get plenty of attention or just because he could afford to dress any way he wanted to."

"Rabbi, I think you hit the nail on the head. Marlen certainly wants our attention and that is probably not a cheap suit he's wearing. I don't particularly care for the color, but it did get my attention."

"Do you guys think he's a gangster"? I asked.

"Well Esther, when I'm playing music in front of a crowd this size, I often dress up accordingly, to be remembered," Melky answered.

"Listen you two; you shouldn't judge a person by the clothes that they wear."

"You're right Rabbi, but they could be making a statement and not necessarily a fashion statement."

"Okay you guys, let's get back to the seminar, and see if Marlen has made a costume change."

CHAPTER 10

BIG VALUABLE ROCKS

When we entered the room the projection screen read;

Passageways to Riches #32
Debt Elimination

"Eliminating debt is like going on a diet.

Eat less and move more;
You should plan your shopping trips;
Don't go food shopping when you are hungry;
Don't be an impulse buyer.

Buy less and save more.

Accumulation of debt leads to monthly fees and interest, possibly superseding your ability to make payments.

It would be easy to say that the basic way to eliminate debt would be to pay off all of your creditors in full. If you make no payments, you are not building any credit ratio muscle. Let's look at credit card debt. This can become problematic, particularly if you are making monthly payments that total three percent or more than the actual debt.

One of the items that a finance company or a bank considers in the decision to give you a loan is called, debt-to-income-ratio. To be eligible for a loan you must qualify by having funds available that are not being used to make payments on other bills.

Be careful not to needlessly fill out credit applications because they will show up on your credit reports, which will make you look like you are applying for loans all over the place. That would raise red flags and you might get T/D'd, or Turned Down for your request.

Before you ever decide to declare bankruptcy, talk to at least two CPA's and at least two lawyers.

Never bite off more than you can chew.

Passageways to Riches #33
Auctions

The biggest and year-round auctions are held online by the Government Services Administration, or GSA. They auction off all kinds of surplus, seizures, forfeited properties etc. of anything and everything including and not limited to:

Automobiles;
Tools;
Cars;
Trucks;
Large and small properties;
Land; etc.

Guess who the biggest landlord is in the United States? Yep, the GSA. If you are interested in buying at auctions, and actually, I recommend that all of you check out their website, GSA Auctions.

I told you, America is on sale right now!

HUD also has auctions on housing and properties where they are willing to take a loss and there is no minimum bid!

There are different types of auctions, particularly those that deal in Real Estate.

Absolute Auctions require no minimum bids. They are risky to the sellers. I once bid on seven properties at one of these and got all seven for 30 cents on the dollar.

Seller Reserve Auctions. These are auctions that the seller has the right to bid and essentially can determine if a bid price is acceptable. They often have their own websites and most anyone is invited. When there is a bad auction, due to poor publicity at a time close to that of the actual auction, it can be a plus if you are a buyer. Check the classified section of your newspapers as a source to find these.

In any auction that you attend, be punctual. You want to sit up front. If you are bashful, you do not belong at an auction and perhaps you may not qualify as an entrepreneur. You need to break that bad habit.

Passageways to Riches #34

Networking

Folks, understand that you have the power to make a difference. In networking, your powers are based upon who you know and not necessarily on what it is that you know. Are you all familiar with the six degrees of separation? It is also known as the human web. In short, it is a theory that you know someone who is no further away than six other people. We are all connected and that applies to the whole world.

I am a friend of a friend of a friend of a friend of a friend that is a friend of yours. With that said, there is a synergistic power in numbers that is huge and exponentially unaccountable. Your old friends, school chums, family, neighbors, colleagues, business prospects, customers, would be excited for you to ask them for their assistance or help. Particularly, if periodically, you touch bases with them and offer your assistance and/or help.

The online social media is also a great tool for you to use sending those in your databases, information related to their fields of business and/or interests. The personal touch is invaluable. Attention is love and every one of us wants to be loved. It only takes seconds to email Joe Shmo, who happens to be a pet lover, an article about pets. What is the value of that?

You can also connect people to other people with like interests. That too has value and neither one of them is likely to forget that it was you who interconnected them.

The secret to networking is, if you have it, flaunt it.

Ladies and gentlemen, for our next subject we are going to need another volunteer. I need to warn you that specifically after this moment our seminar is going to have an effect on you that could change your lives and your perspective on riches. Is that okay with you all?"

After the attendees curiously answered yes, a few hands went up to volunteer. Marlen chose a guy named Charles who happened to be a handsome young man probably in his twenties.

Marlen had this large empty paint bucket on a table in the front of the room. He also had a few sacks of what appeared to be rocks on the table. Marlen then asked Charles to fill the bucket with these rocks. While Charles was filling the bucket, Marlen showed us all a sample of what the rocks looked like. He told us that they averaged about two inches in diameter.

"Is the bucket indeed full?"

"Yes," answered Charles.

Marlen then thanked Charles and asked for a round of applause.

While I wondered where this was going, Marlen asked for yet another volunteer. This time he chose a man named William. He was probably in his late thirties. Marlen had another couple of sacks that now had some pebbles. He showed us a sample again and they were much smaller than the initial two-inch rocks. Marlen then asked William to put as many of the pebbles into the same bucket as possible. William began and every now and then he would cleverly shake the bucket to make room for more of the pebbles.

Marlen again with his wily smile asked William,

"Is that it?, is it full?"

"I don't think I can get any more in there," William answered.

"Let's give William a round of applause."

Now that I was completely mystified, Marlen asked for another volunteer.

He chose a pretty, young gal named Joanne. Again, Marlen had another sack. This time it was sand.

"Joanne, please put as much of this sand into the same bucket."

Joanne was able to get about half of her sack of sand into the bucket even after shaking the bucket like William did.

"Is the bucket full now, Joanne?"

"Yes, I believe so. I don't think I can get another grain in there."

"Let's give Joanne a round of applause."

After the crowd stopped clapping, and I don't know what for, Marlen explained,

"Folks, I want you to imagine that those larger two inch rocks represent those things in life that are most dear to you:

Your health,
Your spouse,
Your children,
Your dearest friends and relatives.

The half-inch pebbles represent the things in life like your house, your jobs, your cars, etc. The sand represents the other things in your lives, the stuff so to speak like your televisions, your cell phones, radios, papers, and all of the stuff that you own. The bucket represents your life. If you were to fill your lives with the stuff, there would be no room for the pebbles and surely no room for the larger rocks. The same holds true that if you fill your lives with the pebbles, there would be no room for what you hold most dear and precious to you."

The screen lit up with,

Passageways to Riches #35
Priorities

This is a lesson in prioritization. You see, being rich, famous, or successful, does not necessarily guarantee that you will be happy. Take for example the successful people like: Ernest Hemmingway, Jimi Hendrix, Janis Joplin, Jim Belushi, Marilyn Monroe, Elvis, and the list goes on and on. They were rich, famous, and successful, but so unhappy that they developed suicidal tendencies.

Being happy is actually a cure for disease and a way to achieve a greater longevity."

That was exactly what Rabbi Cohen told me.

"When you are happy, those around you tend to be happy, as though it was contagious. When you smile at people, they tend to smile back at you.

Take the time to organize and prioritize whatever it is that makes you and your loved ones happy. Isn't it mostly the quality time that you spend with them?

We have to move on everyone and the next subject is,

Passageways to Riches #36
Getting Started

My friends, in the beginning G-D created something from nothing. I realize that I've made that point often throughout the seminar but we were created in the image of G-D and have the ability to create something ourselves out of what appears to be nothing, and once again I say, why not something of value? When you create value, you create wealth.

Have you ever heard of the book or the film, 'Acres of Diamonds'? This true story takes place in South Africa. A farmer was visited by a man who explained that diamonds were being discovered in various locations on the African continent. The farmer was so inspired by his visitor's story that he decided to sell his farm and head out to the diamond lines seeking the riches.

He wandered all over the continent for years searching for the precious stones and wealth, which he never found. Eventually he went broke, threw himself into a river, and drowned. The new owner of the farmer's old farm had an unusual rock on his mantle place that was the size of a rather large egg. A visitor came by, spotted the rock, and excitedly told the new owner of the farm that this was the largest diamond he had ever seen. The owner said that he did not know it was a diamond and said that his whole farm was covered with these rocks, and so it was. The farm turned out to be the richest diamond mine in the world now known as the Kimberly Diamond Mine.

The moral of the story is that each of us has his or her own acres of diamonds that all too often have not yet been discovered. If we focus on and explore what we have and what we know, there is a treasure chest full of opportunity.

In this, the information age, we can share and market much of what we excel in. Every single one of us has a niche. What are yours? Write them down. Tell everyone you know about your intentions and do not expect advice. Your only purpose for sharing with everyone is to make your goals real for yourselves.

To get started on your passageways to riches, you must learn that someday is not any part of the week. I can promise that when you begin to take action, you will take your lives to the next level and probably even higher yet.

Most people are lazy, which is unnatural and requires conditioning. They are addicted to waiting and have no trouble procrastinating. Don't be afraid of beginning a new project. To begin something new, one might take a step into that unexplored region of their experiences. Avoiding that potential pain of doing something you have never done, could take precedence over doing something to achieve your plans.

We are going to move on to another related topic, which is the B.S.

Passageways to Riches #37
B.S. — Belief Systems

We are the sum total of all of our experiences.

We are what it is that we have repeatedly been called and what we call ourselves. We are conditioned to believe the illusions to the allusions and analogies that are not only B.S. but can draw us back and prevent us from moving forward. When we were children it was clear, knowing what we wanted to be when we grew up. However, what happened along the way? What caused us to drag along our baggage and be blinded of the infinite wonderful possibilities for our futures? Why_do we keep replaying the failures of our past and become the victims instead of the active participants to achieve success? What are the causes of our myopia that has hypnotized us from being who we could be instead of just who we are?

When you wake up from your slumber or your sleep, do you affirm to yourself that you are going to have a great, interesting, profitable, healthy day? There is after all, no evidence that you can't, only evidence that you may not have done it yet.

If you should fail, so what the heck. If you do not take the risk to fail, you'll surely never succeed. Smart people do stupid things. That is a part of growth. It is complicated to learn from success but there is much to learn from losing. The simple trick is to pick your keesters back up and learn from your mistakes and/or the mistakes of others. You can also learn from the snake who sheds his skin, becoming rejuvenated and gifted for a positive change in his life.

Society's laziness would never have been tolerated in the days of old. We would have been tortured and beheaded. Welfare, Social Security checks, Unemployment checks, are you kidding?

We cheer and we root for our favorite sports teams and for others to succeed, but what about ourselves? Everyone, I want you to get up from your seats right now and raise your hands like you are number one and cheer for yourselves."

The whole room at this point was coming unglued.

It was so loud I could hardly think. I did have the presence of mind though to cheer for myself, as silly as it appeared.

"People, I want you to realize that you are perfect just the way you are. If you do not believe me, tell your creator that you are dissatisfied, or change yourself. I do understand that the only people wanting a change are babies with dirty diapers. Life won't give you what it is that you may deserve, but it will give you what you claim."

Melky mysteriously darted to the back of the room as soon as Marlen stopped talking. I watched him approach the staff. I was somewhat curious so I took Fred with me as we were about to break for lunch. We stopped at the staff tables where people were swarming. Marlen then yelled out that there would be an hour and a half lunch break. Melky looked perturbed and I asked him what he was talking about to the staff. He said that he was curious about an affiliate to Gandalph Enterprises. He added that he was sent an email invitation to this seminar by an affiliate of theirs called Enoch Enterprises. Before he could finish telling me more, I mentioned that I was also sent an email invitation to the seminar from Enoch Enterprises.

"Well guess what," he asked, "The staff has never heard of Enoch Enterprises."

I asked him how that could be and he said that there are often paid affiliates to web sites that get a commission on a paid per click or paid per sale basis.

"But there was no sale, it was free!" Melky yelled.

The three of us then headed out the doors and waited for an elevator.

Melky said that perhaps if we were to sign up for a future paid event that Enoch Enterprises might get their commission at that time. I thought that was somewhat strange.

While in the glass elevator, Rabbi Fred asked us if we knew who Enoch was. Melky answered that he wouldn't have asked that question to the staff if he had the answer. Rabbi Fred then sarcastically said,

"No, not that Enoch, but the Enoch mentioned in the book of 'Genesis'."

"Isn't he one of the people in the Bible that walked with G-D?" I asked.

Rabbi Fred said,

"Yes, that was the second Enoch mentioned in the Bible. The name Enoch, in the language of the Holy tongue is Chanoch. It is related to the word, chinuch, meaning education."

"You're right Rabbi, and the root is chanach which means to train or educate. The first Chanoch was a son of Cain and Cain named a city with that name. The second Chanoch was the father of Methuselah. It was then at the age of three hundred and sixty-five years that he walked with Hashem (literally-the name, and is used as a name referring to G-D) and G-D took him. That Chanoch was the Great-Grandfather of Noah."

"Wow, you two guys are like a Biblical encyclopedia."

"That's just great, but who can tell me whom Enoch Enterprises are?"

"That is who brought us all together," I said with a laugh. It was a mystery though, but there seemed to be a few mysteries for me at this point.

Fred was sure to get in the last word on the Enoch subject by adding,

"There are several books of Enoch that were found along with the Dead Sea scrolls. The books are seemingly parables accounting for his time spent with G-D and the Angels in Paradise."

CHAPTER 11

AN ANGELIC DISPLAY

When we got down to the hotel lobby we noticed there was an art exhibit spread over half the entire lobby. Glancing at the display we noticed there was a general theme for the exhibit: angels. Melky said this was a sign and he wouldn't be joining us for lunch. He then ran back to the elevators. I told Fred to go ahead without me and I might catch up with him at the restaurant later.

The art exhibit had an array of watercolors, oils, tapestries, and sculptures, all of angels. I found myself interested and ventured further into the exhibit. All of the works varied in age from the Renaissance period thru the 21st century. Almost all the angels had appendages of wings and halos. Their wings were often white and feathery while their halos were white or colors appearing to be crowns of light. Their bodies were human. Some looked child-like and some were adult. I wondered why the artists perceived of angels looking like humans. My own knowledge of angels was rather limited. I did however recognize that one of the oils portrayed Jacob, wrestling with the angel, the story told in the book of 'Genesis'. I remembered that was when his other name, Israel, was given to him. I thought about the meaning of the word Israel, he who strives with G-D. It made me realize that not only am I an Israelite, but so is anyone who strives to understand G-D. This painting looked like Jacob and the angel were intimately dancing with each other instead of fighting with each other as the story explains.

Most of the oils were quite beautiful, having lucid color contrasts, which seemed to provide their own light. By the same token, I felt the angelic theme was rather pedantic, pertaining to the artists perceptions of angels and those of paradise. When I proceeded further, I saw a sculpture titled, 'The Angels, According To Enoch.' That was too coincidental; too much Enoch, which freaked me out, and I decided to leave the exhibit.

I walked a few blocks to the kosher restaurant where they served meat dishes. Fred was sitting near a window facing the street and I joined him. All I had time to order was a dessert which was to faint for. It was a dark chocolate mousse covered with strawberries. If I had time, I would have ordered another.

I told Fred about the Enoch sculpture, which he disregarded, but did say he would check it out. I then asked Fred what he thought about Melky. Fred seemed a little jealous but he seemed to answer with sincerity,

"He appears to know a lot about Torah. He probably has a big heart, he's well mannered, and generally seems like a nice guy. Why do you ask?"

"I think I am attracted to him."

"You think you are attracted to him? Come on Esther, it's me you're talking to. When are you going to find your Beshert and just settle down?"

I smiled and told Fred that he has always been a dear friend of mine and I could always confide in him. We went back to the hotel and while passing the art exhibit I again thought about the coincidence of the Enoch stuff. When we got up to the seminar, Marlen was standing by the doors again greeting every one of us by our names. How on earth could he remember everyone's name? I found Melky and we sat next to him. He looked at me smiling and shaking his head no. I knew that meant he had no further information on who the Enoch affiliate was.

"Okay folks, this spaceship is about to take off so strap yourselves in." The screen lit up again with

Passageways to Riches #38

Accumulation

"The old adage is, 'A penny saved is a penny earned.' If you save that penny for too long it will only be worth a fraction of a cent. Saving money without investing and re-investing is a formula for losing money. Saved money loses its value by at least the rate of inflation. If you have money in a savings account, the inflation rate is much higher than the interest you make on your money and you can bank on that. When investing your money, the longer you have to wait to get back at least your initial investment, the better the discount should be on the amount of the investment. We are back on that subject of time again. Time erodes the dollar value.

If you invest in U.S. Savings Bonds, you pay about $60.00 to get back $100.00 at maturity. If you cash out earlier, you will not get back as much because you will not accrue as much interest if you were to wait for full maturity. Theoretically, using this example, at maturity you will have gained $40.00, which is equal to about 66.67% interest, but over a 20-year period. That amounts to about 3.335% interest per annum. But, it doesn't reach that high until it has become fully mature. The reason for that is because the interest is compounded on the total. Cashing out any earlier, you would have to settle for much less than that 3.335% interest per year. The good news is that your money in government bonds is well secured and relatively liquid. The bad news is that the interest is miniscule.

Holding on to your cash is a loser. Spending your money without proper management is also a loser and an even bigger one. Here is the point: there is a universal law that anything you hoard or hold on to, eventually, will erode. Think about it. This does not only apply to money.

The word currency means to flow. When you act as though you are at the end of the line, pertaining to cash flow, you set yourself up for a loss. By giving back to the Universe, more doors will open for you. This concept can apply to the baggage you carry. By baggage, I am referring to unwillingness to forgive both yourselves and others. If you don't let go of it in this lifetime, you may have to re-live that missed opportunity in another.

Only those big rocks that we spoke of earlier are worth holding on to, never letting go.

Focus, Focus, Focus.

Passageways to Riches # 39
Do You Remember

Do you ever feel as though you are losing your memory? If you do, there are exercises that you can do to sharpen the memory. The file cabinet, which is a section in your mind and inside your physical brain, is a muscle. The nature of muscles is that when you use them they become stronger and when not used, they not only become weaker, but they can become dormant. The term for this inactive state is atrophy. The good news about dormant muscles or muscles that have atrophy is they can become trained and/or re-trained so they can be used again.

Without getting into the subject matter of long-term or short-term memory, we will now cover what we believe to be most important in the realm of business and attaining riches. This particular sub-category of memory has to do with remembering people and their names.

A name is like a vessel and more than often a person's name is related to a person's character. If you try to use the meaning of a name though as a mnemonic device or technique, to recall a person's name, you would have to remember many names and their meanings. In name calling, or I should say, in name recalling, the most powerful mnemonic devices are the silly ones. What stands out most in our minds happens to be what is ridiculous or silly to us.

If you relate the sound of a name to a facial characteristic of a person, and the sillier it is, the easier it will be to remember. When you first meet someone, greet her or him with a handshake. I do not mean that you should shake it violently or out of their sockets, nor squeeze their hand like it was in a vise. Simply, just shake hands. As you do so, make the connection before you let go. Do not let go until your association is made. Everyone, please take off your nametags and place them face down on your tables."

Marlen then went down the first five or six rows of the seminar room, greeting each person with their names. I was shocked and actually thought he might have a special set of contact lenses allowing him to read their names from the backs of their nametags. How silly of me though. I have heard of mnemonic devices before, pertaining to other types of memory. This certainly wasn't magic.

"Folks, realize please that I am not trying to show off but I want you to understand that this technique is powerful. I suggest that you meet and greet some people here at the seminar, shake their hands, and make those associations and connections. It's not only good networking but it's like lifting weights to build up muscle mass.

People want to be remembered, unless of course they are guilty of some crime that you witnessed. Remembering names of people is uplifting and a form of love. It is a form of proof that you value them enough to remember their name. Proving that you do value them will make you more valuable. Practice makes perfect.

Another memory technique we teach in our courses is how to remember numbers. Numbers are more abstract and by substituting numbers with consonants to spell words makes them easy to remember. This is a very old technique, which only takes a short period of time to learn in our courses. A genius can remember six digit figures and our students can remember a hundred numbers backward or forward in minutes! Tell me, would you like to learn some of our memory techniques?

Our courses cover all of the 50 Passageways to riches and in greater detail. Let's move on to,

Passageways to Riches # 40
Franchises

If you want to be in business for yourself and not by yourself, there are two things that you can do. One is to join up with our team and partner with us on some deals and the other is to buy a franchise. In a way, buying a franchise is like buying a j.o.b., but it does have an upside. You can follow in the footsteps of those who have already proven that their businesses perform well. Documented accounts are available and accessible to any franchise owner prospects. What you want to look for are familiar brands with positive track records. Start-up costs could be prohibitive and frankly, that's why we prefer to use our own noggins to create our own businesses. Out of our own established businesses, we can eventually sell franchises.

I have a friend who built up a business doing tax accounting. He built a profitable and recession proof business where he hires student accountants to prepare taxes. He then has a CPA proofread the taxes and they're done. He also sells insurance for automobiles, trucks, motorcycles, health, life (whole life and term), renters, and business. Guess who does my taxes and gives me great rates for bundled up insurance policies? Yep, but I also do some proofreading before anything is filed. I always check comparables on the insurance policies regarding premiums and coverage. My friend is now selling franchises in his business and he is making a killing. My advice to him was to create a brand name that people will remember.

My dear friends, before you convert any ideas you have that can transform into franchises, or even businesses for that matter, there is a matter of the utmost importance you need to consider. We refer to it as CYA. This brings us to our next passageway.

Passageways to Riches # 41
Asset Protection

CYA means to **C**over **Y**our **A**ss-ets. Riches will most often come from your entrepreneurial skills. You will use your skills to create businesses having the potential to make large sums of money. Regardless of your particular niche, you must realize the source of these riches come from the first law of the manifestation process. That is simply, Thought. Your own ideas preciously come to you and they are your own property. Much like owning many or any properties, you should protect them. They actually have value, at least potential value.

My point here is to get you to understand your ideas are like precious stones and you would not want to risk losing them without some form of insurance, protecting their values. There are countless tragic stories how amassed fortunes went into the hands of others merely because ideas were not protected. Ideas are intellectual property. They include: Knowledge, information, inventions, patents, designs, data, trademarks, copyrights, and even reputations. These are just a few you should recognize and not take for granted, just because they came from you. You are a riches magnet and the sooner you realize that, the sooner you will have those riches, which also need to be protected and sheltered.

You must also realize that your ideas are potential liabilities. We are looking for assets. Of course, the best way to protect your assets will be to consult your personally trusted lawyers.

Our team of professionals has a nationwide team of lawyers available, 24/7. Whenever we get a brainstorm or have a problem, all we need to do is make a phone call, and help is on its way. Speaking about on its way, we must advance."

Passageways to Riches #42
KISS Method

When I saw what was on the screen all I could ponder was the current state of my libido. I couldn't wait to hear this. I was probably hoping to learn a new kissing technique.

"Right here folks, within this high-tech complex world, lay a major secret. As complex as it is, we are still experimenting and doing research on even more advanced technologies. The stresses related to all of this searching, which takes hours, days, weeks, months, and sometimes years, limit our ability to kiss.

Keep **I**t **S**imple **S**weetie.

Go ahead and laugh. Truthfully, the endless time of laborious testing, formulating, and researching has caused much pain in this world. I believe in the application of the real scientific method, but because we are so advanced at this particular and auspicious time, we have forgotten about those fundamentals.

Science strives with cause and effect. A question is asked and then research is done. A hypothesis is then formulated and tested by experimentation. The data is then analyzed and the tricky part is to draw a conclusion. Does it have the same result all of the time or just once in a while?

When you are on the passageways to riches, if you invest your time or money and have a negative result, expecting a positive result with the same action would be insane. Wake up! Do it differently or do something else. Doing what others have successfully done and in the exact same manner, you can expect the same results. Let me break it down.

The rudiments of attaining riches begin with the appreciation of earning your first penny. You see, if you have a hundred dollars, you have ten thousand pennies. If you are looking to earn a thousand dollars, then you want to earn one million pennies. Breaking it down into a smaller increment, rather than meant to intimidate you, it is meant to focus your attention on that first earned, shiny red cent. The analogy here is that you usually can't arrive at answers to apparent difficult problems without dissecting them into simpler and more basic questions.

Once, I became puzzled why my charming wife was so angry with me. She remained that way far too long and it escalated to the point of my seeking out help from a family therapist. First of all, never be afraid to ask for help. I phoned him and he scheduled me in right away to meet at his office. His office was a small room within his own home. When I got there, I wanted to ask him if he was renting or buying this beautiful home. I am always networking, looking for buyers and sellers, wherever I go. On this particular occasion though, I decided to stay focused on why I was there.

When we sat down in his office the first thing he said was,

"What is your problem?" I had to think about that for a moment because I didn't feel like it was my problem. There certainly was a problem that I at least shared. I did not want to sound like a big fool so I eloquently answered that my wife is going crazy. She harps at me relentlessly the moment I get home from work.

With a smirk on his face, he said that it sounds like I am the one who is going crazy. I agreed and then he looked at me as if I was wasting his time. He asked me to break it down and be more precise. I told him that my wife has all these ridiculous problems and it is as if she throws them all into a pile, gets overwhelmed, and then takes it out on me.

I was shocked to find this professional therapist begin laughing. The situation I was in, I explained, was far from being funny. His expression then became serious. He then explained,

"Please forgive me for having laughed but I need to explain that aside from being a therapist, I am also a Rabbi and teach Kabala to Rabbinical students. Just today, I happened to be teaching a Kabalistic concept that is much related to your problem. Women live in a realm known as Binah. Literally, it means understanding, and comes from the root, binyan, meaning to build. Men live in a realm called Chochmah, which literally means wisdom. Having chochmah can give men natural capabilities to receive thoughts or ideas. That is not to say that either sex is incapable of the others potential to understand or receive ideas, but those are the natural and inherent realms for the sexes. Now when the two are combined, working together in complimentary fashion, the potential for development becomes extraordinary. The woman is capable of taking your smallest idea or desire and makes it real by development."

Now I was a little perplexed but found this rather interesting. He continued to tell me,

"Think about it like this, when you give a woman a tiny little seed, unseen by the naked eye, no pun intended, she holds on to this seed, nurtures it, and

Out comes a big baby!"

When he screamed, "out comes a big baby," I started laughing and began to appreciate his humor. He explained that this is a natural event and it is within her nature to magnify, intensify, amplify, and enhance. He said that I should be willing to help her with my wisdom by sorting out and tackling one problem at a time, in a simple and orderly manner. He then stood up, shook my hand and wished me good luck, nodding affirmatively that if I heeded to his advice, all will be well and good. Again, I thought about networking but first things first.

When I got home my wife was about to cry, so overwhelmed with her issues. I couldn't help but smile and tell her how much I appreciated and loved her. I hugged her and gave her a great big kiss. I sat her down with a piece of paper, a pen, and asked her to help me, help her, solve her problems in a simple and orderly manner. After about twenty minutes, she melted into my arms, sat on my lap, and the rest I cannot reveal but it began with a KISS and it was wonderful.

I think that pretty much explains the KISS method but hey fellas, you are not exempt from complicating matters, particularly if you live in this realm, which the Kabala refers to as wisdom. Just remember to KISS."

Passageways to Riches #43
Motivation

Before I could get myself motivated, I was still in a state of shock. I was learning a concept from Kabala, taught by a man who looked like a gangster, and he explained the concept better than I ever heard it before. I felt ready to be motivated!

"Everyone, please listen. We are going to have our staff hand something to all of you. Please keep it in front of you and wait for instructions."

I couldn't wait to see what they were going to give to us. I was hoping for hundred dollar bills yet somehow I had an unusual expectation it would be something even more valuable. It turned out to be a piece of thread with a not so precious metal charm tied to one end of it that said, Gandalph Open Seminars Training.

"Okay everyone, one of the things we teach is a process we call Natural Psycho-Neural Physiology, NPNP. I'll explain later."

I felt like I was a psycho for expecting a hundred bucks.

"Please follow my directions. First, everyone exhale deeply and then take a deep breath. Now hold it, hold it, and exhale. Let's do that one more time. Exhale, deep breath, hold it, hold it, exhale, and feel relaxed."

When I took that second deep breath, it made my head begin to spin faster than it was already spinning.

"I want you all to hold up the thread with the charm at the bottom. You can rest your elbows on the tables in front of you. Good, now holding your hand still, concentrate on your mind moving the charm side-to-side like a pendulum. Concentrate on it moving from side-to-side. Focus your mind moving the charm side-to-side.

Good, now concentrate on your mind moving the charm forward and back, forward and back. Focus people, forward and back.

Good, now concentrate deeply on your mind moving the charm in a clockwise circle. Don't look at anyone else; just concentrate on the charm moving in a clockwise direction. Nothing else exists but your mind moving the charm in a clockwise direction.

Excellent, now concentrate on your mind moving the charm in a counter-clockwise direction. Nothing else exists but your mind moving the charm in a counter-clockwise direction. You can do it people, counter clockwise. Awesome!"

I couldn't believe it. I felt like I was being hypnotized. I intentionally held my hand still but the charm was moving in every direction that Marlen had commanded.

"Well allrighty then, let's give yourselves a big round of applause. You see, in this process of Natural Psycho-Neural Physiology, basically, your conscious mind sends a signal to your sub-conscious mind. Your physical body then follows suit. It is that simple and can be used as a motivational stimulus. If you concentrate on something you want to do, no matter how difficult, your sub-conscious mind commands all of the body's cells and muscles to move in that direction. I didn't hypnotize you, you did it to yourselves, and your bodies took action. This is a form of mental programming. What you focus on expands.

Before you go to bed and when you first wake up, focus on something you want to accomplish that particular day. Then write it down. It could be something you might forget about or avoid in the course of a busy day, but do it. Practice makes perfect and your commands will progress.

Positive thinking is preceded by possibility and probability thinking. You can accomplish anything you think. What you may have to do is a mere paradigm shift to convince yourselves that you are more powerful than you think you are. Remove the word impossible from your vocabularies. Do this! Information without implementation is useless.

It says in the Bible that for G-D, nothing is impossible. Even if your parents didn't plan you, you were planned by G-D. You are definitely not a coincidence. Everyone was made from nothing into something. We were all created in the image of G-D. We have the ability to take a mere thought and turn it into something tangible. Why not something good, having value?

There are two driving forces to almost everything we do. They are pleasure and pain. Fear and doubt are each related to pain. They are distracting to positive movement. Doubt is the easy cop-out based on your B.S. Fear is that **F**alse **E**vidence **A**ppearing **R**eal. Doubt is an acronym for **D**ucking, **O**r **U**nwisely **B**eing **T**roubled. It can escalate to the realm of fear. For example, when you are in a very dark room, fear may overcome you. The reason being, you don't know what else is in the room. It is that not knowing which evolves from doubt and fear into pain. This is true both physically and spiritually. We are all capable of our bodies generating and emitting bio-photons, which are sparks of light. Given just a tiny spark of light when it is very dark, there becomes a great illumination. The more light that is shone, the more the details become unraveled, revealed, and understood. When that happens, the pain from the doubt and fear will diminish and disappear. Again, this is true both physically and spiritually.

My friends, motivation can be a uniquely individual force. Everyone is different and what motivates some of us can de-motivate others. Unfortunately, anger is one of those self-destructive motivators. Drug addicts are motivated to do drugs. Alcoholics are motivated to drink alcohol. Your perception of what you are is a factor to what motivates you. It is powerful enough to propel you forward, which many of us choose for a motivational lift. What we might overlook are the responsibilities and repercussions. There are a myriad of better tools to use for motivation. What we have shared with you so far is universal. Our courses delve into the depths, in detail, to help you understand those personal driving forces that can move you past any and all barriers between you and attaining anything or everything you want.

"Well folks, this weekend seminar is just about over so let's get that blood rushing in order to have the energy and attention needed to finish with your maximum potential for ingesting material that will bring you riches. Everyone, please stand up."

That thought brought a smile to my face. This was timely and just what the doctor ordered. We all stood up. As I did so, I could feel my joints cracking and popping. Marlen had us all exhale and once again, take a deep breath. He repeated that command and then had us do something, which I found quite profound.

"Folks, most people, throughout the course of a busy day, forget to breathe. That is a fact. Even when we do breathe, we don't do it properly in a manner of sending healing messages to all the parts of our wondrous powerful bodies. You want to take deep breaths, periodically, by holding your thumb on your navel with your fingers pointing downward. Try it. Notice that your stomach is expanding. Picture your stomachs, in your mind, being an inner tube, which is inflating. Watch the clean air circulate to all the body parts below your torsos. By using this method of taking deep breaths, you are less likely to send too much oxygen to your brain and this will help you have fewer headaches and a better psychological outlook. We will explore that a little later. Now while you are standing, raise your right hand and point your index finger to the chandelier above you."

While I was peering at the crowd, Marlen instructed Max,

"Your other right hand, Max, so you won't be slugging your neighbor."

When I chuckled, Marlen gave us another command to twirl our hand in a clockwise motion covering the periphery or the outside edge of the chandelier.

"Clockwise, Norman," Marlen corrected.

Again, I chuckled, wondering why people don't know their right hand from their left or the direction the hands move on a clock.

"Now very slowly, bring your hands all the way down as far as you can without bending your bodies, continuing to move your hands in a clockwise motion or a helix, like a circular staircase."

While I was thinking about how much I loved circular and spiral staircases, following these simple commands, I was watching Marlen demonstrate what he was commanding us to do. I noticed something peculiar that caused me to look at my own twirling hand and finger, which was now at the same level of my stomach.

"What direction are your fingers now circling, clockwise or counter-clockwise?"

Some of the people including myself were in a state of disbelief, watching our hands still twirling, now apparently, in a counter-clockwise direction.

"Go ahead and sit back down because this unrealistic reality brings us to our next confused passageway to riches.

Passageways to Riches #44
Reality

Reality is merely a perception. For many of you, reality is even more tangible than real estate. Your realities are created by a validation, or an experience that you have had. Your senses however, can be hampered by these validations. Everyone has the potential to be flexible, meaning that your reality can be altered or changed. Your realities are actually related to your dreams.

We are trained to see only what we believe is possible. Not seeing what might actually be in front of us is simply denial. You may be seated next to an angel with wings and halos, like I happened to notice at the art exhibit in the hotel lobby. But, if you are not accustomed to accepting that, your five senses, also trained to your realities, won't be able to acknowledge him or her, or should I say, it.

Reality is controlled by your limited past experiences. Reality is a multiple choice where multiple possibilities exist, but only in our sub-conscious mind. A person with a completely and truly opened mind is rare. Now here is where it gets interesting. A pilot flying an airplane going from point A to point B has a course heading. In order to fly to his destination he must constantly change his course heading by being flexible due to unpredictable wind and weather changes.

Being flexible allows you to set new courses and experience more and new realities. Increasing your spectrum of reality can be most rewarding. Pleasure and pain are very real to you. Fear representing pain in many cases is again that **F**alse **E**vidence **A**ppearing **R**eal and can make you feel out of control. When you come to realize that you are an integral part of this glorious universe, you'll realize that you are perfect just the way you are. When you are grateful for being you, it will enable you to experience and pass through your pains, giving them far less longevity. Your pleasures then will be enhanced and given a greater longevity. Now tell me, who doesn't want that?

A very useful tool for you is acting out the attribute of humility. By being humble, which is a downsizing of the ego, can be compared to the splitting of the atom. In physics and quantum physics, we learn that the smaller parts of the atom are even more powerful than the atom itself. This appears contradictory to the concept of holism, which says that the whole is greater than the sum of its parts. Essentially, there is no contradiction. We learn that the smaller parts are indeed unique, having powerful pure abstract potential. By being humble, we become opened up to this anomaly also known as the quantum wave function. It is also called an entanglement and is a connection to the universal whole. An enormous, and perhaps, infinite amount of energy exists through this consciousness.

We have routines that scientists say accustom ourselves to using only as much as ten percent of our brain, maybe even less when coming to grips with reality. Our five senses can play tricks on us in a unique process that actually is our own self-defense mechanism. We are being self-protected from sources in our brains that think anything out of the ordinary is dangerous. Sometimes it is strong enough to experience what is not real or will not let us experience what is real. The environment of the mind is no different than the infinite environment of the universe. We are capable of four billion thoughts per second and yet we only capture as many as two thousand bits per second. This limiter is a part of your brain and is called the visual cortex. It is the computer that processes your reality. It will not allow you to see what you cannot comprehend. You want to know that your eyes are the window to your soul. However, in reality, they are like a camcorder filming what they see. Editing takes place in the visual cortex and the information is shared in the other neural cortexes of your mind.

Tell me; is anyone here familiar with space-time geometry?"

One nerdy looking young guy raised his hand.

"Awesome Howard, then you probably know about the connection between time reversal symmetry or asymmetric influence, a ubiquitous theory that the future can be at cause for the present and or the past."

Howard had a non-committal stare that somehow displayed an affirmation of acceptance.

"People, what part of you is eternal? Everything and everyone has a unique purpose, everything else changes. You are indeed perfect the way you are.

Water is the most receptive of the four elements, Water, Air, Fire, and Earth.

We are composed of about 90% water. Realize that your thoughts and prayers are extremely powerful and miracles do exist. Miracles for some are regular everyday occurrences to others. The setbacks to not experiencing miracles are our tenacious fears and our feeling unworthy.

Fiddlesticks, I say!

Stay open.

What you want to hear may not be as valuable as what you will hear.

Friends, I would like to tell you a story of a very powerful surprising experience and lesson I once had as a child. Is that okay with you?"

I found it surprising Marlen was even asking us. He had however, showed signs of being compassionate, intellectual, philosophical, and even spiritual, which made him more interesting but more perplexing as the seminar, moved on. The room was in agreement to listen to another one of his stories.

"When I was about seven years old, my Father and I would have a bonding night once a week. That was the night my Mother would be out playing cards with her sisters. Being a black sheep of sorts, he would take me to places that were beyond any of my own realities and experiences. He would take me to see foreign films and documentaries, beatnik coffee houses to listen to poetry, the old-time silent movie theatre, or we would just stay home to study science, which was certainly his greatest love. My Dad was a genius and I am not just saying that. He spoke fourteen languages and could carry a conversation on just about any subject matter in any one of those languages. I wish I were more like him.

One of Dad's businesses was rebuilding auto transmissions. One particular Wednesday evening, Mom's card night, Dad had to pick up some tranny parts, that's slang by the way for transmission parts. They were left with the mother of one of his suppliers. When we got to her apartment she invited us in. She was probably in her eighties or nineties. Much of her furniture was covered in plastic but she sat us down and made a cup of tea for my Dad. I refused the tea and I am still not much of a teetotaler to this day. They had some conversation and I was frankly a little bored. Eventually when we were about to leave, she had a brainstorm. She remembered having some dried fruit and raw nuts to offer me. As a seven year old, the only treats that I was interested in were chocolate bars. When I was about to refuse, Dad gave me a discreet camel kick that I understood. It meant that I was to do just the opposite, and so, I accepted the dried fruit and raw nuts. As she scurried to the kitchen, I looked at Dad with an expression of why, and he held up his index finger meaning, just wait. She scurried back to meet us and handed me a waxed paper bag filled with dried fruit and raw nuts. When we got to the car, she was still standing in her doorway and waved goodbye. We waved to her and off we went.

Dad then shocked me saying he didn't care if I threw the bag out of the car window. I knew that couldn't be right because Dad taught me that it was a sin to waste. He then explained that by taking something that this old woman was offering to me, I was actually giving her something. He explained that no one pays much attention to her and not many go to visit her. By taking something that she had to offer me, I was actually giving her something. This was a very profound lesson for me that I will never forget. As we drove away, I started eating the stuff and it was pretty darn good. She actually made the dried fruit herself. I polished it all off before we even got back home. The lesson here is that taking is a form of giving and that is our next subject.

Passageways to Riches #45
Give and Take

The universe is like the bank. If you want to borrow or take something from it, you must put up some sort of collateral. There is a universal law in balance. You can always take out but you have to put something back in. Measure for measure is how we continue to grow. There are apparent dichotomies like:

Black or White,
Good or Bad,
Right or Left,
Give or Take,
Addition or Subtraction,
Multiplication or Division,
Better or Worse,
Richer or Poorer,
Winning or Losing,
Borrowing or Lending,
Listening or Speaking,

Wealth or Poverty.

The list goes on. For every action there is supposedly an equal and opposite reaction. All of these dichotomies are actually only perceptions. Your neural associations to these perceptions are what give them the power over you. Blessings can come in disguises. What may appear as intolerable pain may unfold and transform into ecstatic bliss. So overwhelmed am I about the blessings I focus on, leaves me no time to be caught up in my shortcomings. Observing what you perceive as the good will create a strong anchor for you to build on.

The way to a compelling future is knowing you give to get and you get, to get what you want. What you get by giving is pleasure,

Realize your growth up until now,
Give back to the universe by being grateful, and give thanks.
Pay it forward and do random acts of kindness.

That is how your plates will be filled. Be careful with the thoughts that you give out and be more careful with your speech. Think good and it will be good.

When you give, do so in a manner that does not put you on a pedestal above your gift's recipient. Realize your growth and your contribution. Have a compelling future knowing what you give back is what creates the longevity. Give anonymously, and realize, the universe knows and remembers.

Passageways to Riches #46
Passion

The enjoyment of life coupled with the ability to touch those around you and by doing so will help you focus on your passion. Not taking advantage of others nor sabotaging your relationships, you stand alongside those that represent goodness. When you are passionate about something and you know it is good, doors will open for you, and in ways like you never imagined.

If your goal is only to make lots of money, remember that cash can be petty, the almighty dollar is getting weaker, and for some, it may find a need to be laundered.

The questions are:

What makes you better?
What makes your neighborhood better?
What makes your city, your state, your country, and your world a better place?

These are the things you can do which will amass you great fortunes.

One of the things you can do is what I remember a blind woman doing. She could see better and was able to see what the human eye could not see. She was able to see kindness and goodness in some of the little things that people do. She, herself, was appreciative even having been dealt a bad hand by losing her eyesight. Her vision though, metaphorically became far more acute.

There is a law in physics also found in Zen philosophy amongst other places. If a vessel is full, then there is no room to put anything else inside of it. This is likened to the mind, where someone so full of himself or so set in his ways, cannot be open to learn and/or receive any more. Worse than that is to change. The only people that are not afraid and want a change, are babies with dirty diapers.

Is a glass half-empty or half-full? The optimist will say that it is half-full. The pessimist will argue that it is half-empty. What the heck is the difference? If it is the mind we are dealing with, and it's half-empty, that's excellent because it alludes to the possibility of there being sufficient space to add new and additional information to it. When it is half-full, then it seems more limited as to how much more it can accept.

The difference between the mind and the heart, at least metaphorically, is when you have an empty heart; there may be no room for warmth or kindness. A full heart expands and has room for everything. When the heart and the mind work in conjunction with each other, a phenomenal powerhouse is formed. Include the heart in your decision-making, and you will become passionate.

When you love what you are doing, you will be prone to excel at it. Whatever the compensation is for what you are doing represents pleasure and pleasure is the greater part of your reward. I may sound a bit altruistic, but let's look at this scientifically. When you love what you are doing, you are altering the very concept of time and defying gravity! Have you ever noticed when you are with someone you love or are doing something you love, how fast time flies? I use the term fly, because that is what you are doing, defying gravity. On the other hand, when you are with someone that you would rather not be with, or doing something you really would rather not be doing, how slowly time crawls. That is when you are bogged down by gravity."

Marlen, who transformed into a preacher of sorts had me fired up. I had the urge to defy time with Melky. Marlen continued preaching,

"I must also point out the importance of humor. There is a need to incorporate humor at times, even when you are up against some of the greatest obstacles and roadblocks in your quest for success.

I recently met with your very own former Mayor and Governor, Rudy Giuliani. When he first became Mayor, he formed an office for emergency management. The scope of that office was to coordinate emergency efforts for gas attacks, plane crashes, and suicide bombings. Of course, on 9/11 no one was totally prepared, particularly for hijacked commercial jets turning into guided missiles aimed at the two largest and most populated buildings in New York.

There was a response to the attack, which did actually save thousands of lives. When Giuliani was informed how many lives were lost, he was shocked. He tried to compare this type of a catastrophe, to a comparable one in recent history. What he came up with was the Blitzkrieg in London during World War II. At that time, the Blitzkrieg shocked London with relentless bombings. Winston Churchill was then the Prime Minister of England. Churchill managed to fire up the spirit of the British people by frequently delivering positive thoughts and prayers to the populace over radio broadcasts. That was the lesson.

Giuliani told me that he only remembered a few things that stood out in his mind about Winston Churchill. Once, here in Manhattan, Churchill was invited to a luncheon. He attended and happened to be seated next to Lady Astor. The locals that set up the seating arrangement apparently did not realize that Lady Astor, although British herself and a former member of Parliament, was no fan of Churchill, nor was he a fan of hers. Both Churchill and Astor were well known to be witty sorts. Churchill was known to have a few belts on occasion and I don't mean the kind that keep your britches on your waist. He had a few at this luncheon and Lady Astor accused him of being drunk. Churchill turned to face Lady Astor and he said,

"You're right. I am drunk, and in the morning, I will look in the mirror, splash some water on my face, and proceed to business as usual. In the morning, you will look in the mirror and you will still be ugly."

Another Lady Astor and Churchill story known to Giuliani was Lady Astor telling Churchill,

"If you were my husband, I'd poison your tea," to which he responded,

"Madam, if you were my wife, I would drink it!"

A few days after 9/11 President Bush arrived at Ground Zero in a helicopter. There was a line of people that he would greet from the FDNY, NYPD, clergymen, rescue workers, and last but not least, a construction worker. Now as you all probably know, construction workers here in New York, are some pretty big fellas. As President Bush moved down the line, shaking hands, he finally confronted the construction worker. A bit reluctant to having his hand squeezed by the owner of a bodily frame, about six foot four and weighing around three hundred pounds, the construction worker spread out his arms, hugged the President, and lifted him off the ground. In the heat of the moment a secret service agent, standing next to Giuliani, turned to Giuliani and bitterly interjected,

"If he hurts the President, you're out!"

Giuliani smiled at the secret service agent and said,

"At least it will be out of love."

When times are tough and obstacles are being dealt with on a serious note, it is also important to keep things in perspective and sometimes a little humor is warranted.

When you are passionate about something, you are capable of converting the ordinary into the extraordinary. Give yourself permission to live an extraordinary life.

Help others. Coaching is everything. There is a saying,

'If you feed a person a fish, you'll feed him for a day. If you teach him how to fish, you'll feed him for a lifetime.'

Give to others more than what you're asking for. Hurt people can hurt people. What you focus on expands.

Remember we are here to help you. Ask questions, speak to our staff, and enjoy.

Learning to forgive is paramount to good health and a free mind to become passionate. By freeing up the mind, you are clearing passageways leading to infinity. Removing the baggage your mind needlessly carries is the emotional equivalent to going to the bathroom. Not letting go can compare to being constipated. The longer that occurs, the more dangerous it can become. Not letting go of the baggage, which only exists in your mind anyhow, will clog up your thinking and your positive development. It can literally stop you from getting the finer things out of life. Life can get messy enough, so just clean it up. Let the past be the past. Learn from your mistakes, and that my friends, is called growth.

Understand that neither poverty nor wealth alone will bring you happiness. What is it that gives you positive motivation? What do you want to do? Why do you want to do it? What is your true purpose in life?

Manifest that. Be excellent, you're already perfect. The greater you value yourself, the more the world will value you.

Healing

In order to be at the top of your game you want to be healthy. Feeling good allows you to operate at full potential. If there is a routine you have that energizes and makes you feel well, stick with it. The things we did when we were young allowed us to be agile. It's the lack of movement that ages us. Getting older is not the problem; it is the lack of focus on movement, which culminates into making us unproductive.

Almost all of the ancient far eastern martial arts teach proper breathing techniques. We have not only forgotten how to breathe but many of us go on about our lives not even taking notice that we are breathing. The optimal breathing technique is to take fifteen-minute periodic breaks during the course of a day. Focus your attention on sending oxygen to all the parts of your body. That includes your bones, your tendons, your joints, and most importantly, your heart and brain. The brain is the choir conductor that has an important role in sending messages to all the body parts. Those messages that you send can be any that you choose. In other words, your focus and attention to send healthy messages to all of these parts is what can keep everything in optimal working order. It almost sounds too simple but that is a major secret to great health.

Another well-kept simple secret is to help others and heal others. That alone will heal you. As crazy as that may sound, we have a great need for healing others and healing everything else in the universe! The secret of all secrets is that you have the power to do so. Acts of generosity, empathy, and compassion with others will improve your own physical and mental health.

Originally, our healers were spiritual and religious leaders. That led to separation by default and then wars actually broke out over how to heal. Science eventually got into the mix and allopathic forms of healing took precedence. These forms are the most popular today but they can be more invasive than necessary. Homeopathic remedies are now more popular than ever before. We are finally starting to use them often and even for the cures of serious diseases. The word disease is simply dis-ease.

We only have time here to teach you how to heal others using some simple, yet effective techniques. The pre-requisites for almost any types of healing are:

Love,
Gratitude,
Presence,
Mastery.

Love is the true desire to focus your attention and intention to heal others. **Gratitude** is the requirement that shows you are thankful for the opportunity to help and heal others. **Presence** is required and it means your presence of mind. You can heal others who are physically great distances away from you. **Mastery** is the certainty, the knowing, without doubt or fear, that you are capable of healing others.

There is a new branch of science called noetic science. Noetic science has to do with intention. There are many modalities of healing that fall under this category. Intention healing is currently being researched but there is a long list of people and animals that have been cured of the most deadly diseases, simply by a healer's intention.

Diagnosis is not necessary and actually undesirable when you are healing someone using energy or frequency techniques. Diagnosis is a Greek word having the root di- meaning two, and gnosis- meaning not known. Interesting that the word really means two who do not know, neither the patient nor the diagnostician. Not knowing is however a good starting point. From the state of not knowing, it allows the space to learn and eventually know. It is that empty vessel or the open mindedness necessary for a good diagnostician. Since most of us are not diagnosticians there is nothing for us to diagnose. Energy or frequency healing is most effective when we let the universal consciousness and wisdom, do the diagnosing. All we need to do is have the focus and intention to receive the healing powers or energies ourselves and to have our subjects in mind so they can receive the wave patterns, whatever those may be. Science is starting to catch up by learning and proving what we know already to be true.

We teach many different proven techniques in our courses. Unfortunately we do not have time for teaching all of them here. We need to move on.

Passageways to Riches #48
Failure

Out of the hundreds of deals I have done, some have gone south. What makes me happy is the fact that I am always willing to learn, whether it be by my gains or my losses. Every day has a dawn and dusk. The next day will have the same, G-D willing, and again I will seek happiness. That next day I may choose to liquidate any losses, lick my wounds, and in the arena of real estate, I may donate those properties to some worthy people.

In the event that I profit on a deal, I am cautious, because while in pursuit of a dream, if all my energy is on that one dream, and that is all this one dream entails, when it is achieved, what else is there to live for? Expand your dreams and follow up with more. What makes me most happy is what I want to share with all of you here.

In the dictionary, failure is defined as an omission, neglect, or a not doing. It can also mean deception or to fall short. Now the beauty of failure is, without its potential, you cannot succeed. For example, the main factor Communism in Russia and the Berlin Wall collapsed was that there was no opportunity for failure.

Failure and success are actually twins and you cannot arrive at one without the possibility of arriving at the other. Because some people fear failure, they will not even attempt success. The most successful people of all time have had failures. It is not a space to be stuck in and you won't unless you throw in the towel. There are those people who quit because of their BS, yeah, their belief systems, which taught them to buy into the bad. The bad is what sells the news and that negativity is what we have been brainwashed with, since we were young.

In 1981, the Los Angeles Dodgers baseball team, had a playoff and season ending loss to the Huston Astros. Tommy Lasorda was the manager of that Dodger team. He was interviewed on the Larry King radio show after the game. From listening to him and his enthusiasm, you would have thought that the Dodgers won the game. Larry King asked him how he could sound so happy. His answer was,

"The best day in my life is when I manage a winning game and the second best day in my life is when I manage a losing game."

His love for what he did explains his longevity as a manager of a major league baseball team and in a high profile city like Los Angeles.

In one of the late Rocky Balboa films, Rocky tells his son,

"In boxing, it aint how hard you can hit, it's how hard you can get hit and keep on pushing forward."

Having been a non-professional baseball and football coach myself, I learned a lot about how to win by suffering losses. Failures can teach you how to win and be successful. In sports or playing any kinds of games, there is more fun to be had if you enter to play when you realize you can't lose. If having fun is the goal how can you lose? Those are called win-win games.

There is much to learn by your own failures or the failures of others. Failures are an integral part of the learning curve. The passageways to riches are not a straight and narrow path. Many adjustments must be made like steering a car or flying an airplane. Experience teaches, when you make an adjustment, you anticipate a particular result. In most cases the result involves the repetition of an act that had a similar result. If you are looking for your misplaced keys in one location and you keep searching for them in that same location, do not expect them to miraculously appear. If you keep doing what you have always done, you'll keep getting what you have always gotten. Expecting anything else is insanity.

Folks, our team, and organization are constantly making adjustments in order to perfect what we teach you. We therefore strive for perfection in this world of truth. Truth is constant and the only thing constant in this world is change, other than G-Dliness. We have made mistakes and we can spare you from repeating those mistakes.

Learn from the kangaroo who only steps forward. He cannot go backwards. He can move in circles but only moving forwards while balanced by his tail.

I don't want to dwell on failure so I'll end with this. There are no guarantees that you will succeed in anything you do. However, if you are not willing to take risks, calculated risks, where you can possibly fail, you probably won't succeed. Measure your risks and avoid as many failures as possible. Constructive thinking is how to turn a loss into a gain. Realize this:

We live in a world that is messy, unpredictable, incomprehensible, unbelievable, and incredibly interesting.

Our penultimate subject is,"

Passageways to Riches #49

Success

When success lit up on the PowerPoint projection screen, I thought that this might be the moment I've been waiting for. I was trying to digest all the information already thrown at us and realized how powerful it was. It was also eerie that Marlen said the exact same thing that the Indian or the Native American Apache chief, said about change. Were Marlen and Rabbi Aryeh one and the same? Did Marlen have ESP?

"Failure and success are exceedingly related in the balance of nature and super nature. Success can be a successor to failure. You could skip that order and achieve success from wherever you are currently at simply by finding your own definition of success, and doing so with precision. Everyone and everything has a purpose in life. How do you define yours? You are all unique and special. Why are you here?

We here at Gandalph Open Seminars Training, teach a formula for success. It is:

Perception
Gratitude
Dream
Achievability
Plan
Must Do.

In business, do not **perceive** the economy as unattractive. Have you ever noticed how people from foreign countries come here and almost overnight, get rich? Why is that? Well, they are confident. Their BS, yes, their belief systems have told them that here in this United States, there are streets of paved gold, and it offers opportunity for those that take action. Well, you know what? they're right. We are the ones that are spoiled and have been brainwashed and led into believing that life is so complicated and difficult. One can hardly find a job that pays minimum wages. Minimum wages, here in this country. Do you realize how fortunate and privileged we are to live here in this great country? We earn an average of ninety-nine percent more than the rest of the world! That is a fact. There are countless people in many third world countries trying to live on two dollars a day.

You will never earn more than your financial self-image will allow. Money is never a problem nor is the lack of it.

It is the nature for each one of you to be rich and wealthy, setting you here in this room, apart from the masses. The actualization comes when you create the opportunity to take action. Not taking action is likened to the dangerous state of a fish jumping out of the water, which can be gobbled up by the masses in search of a free lunch.

There are countless permutations dictating unforeseen opportunities and threats as well. All you need to do is correct your vision.

After perception comes **gratitude**. Being thankful for what you now have has a supernatural affect, which minimizes the full glass of water enabling you to have more. I use water metaphorically, because of all the four elements; water, air, fire, and earth, water is the most receptive. By the way, be thankful for water. It is the most powerful force on earth and we couldn't live without it. Gratitude is the key that unlocks the door to receive more. Being grateful for what you have releases the resistance to having more and what you resist tends to persist. Have you ever played with a Chinese finger puzzle?"

While half of the room was smirking as though they knew what a Chinese finger puzzle was, I pondered the initials of **G**andalph **O**pen **S**eminars **T**raining, **GOST**. While rehearsing the play, 'The King And The Servant', I learned that gost was the old English spelling for ghost. Did he create this acronym intentionally? Marlen explained the other puzzle,

"You stick a finger from each hand into the woven cylindrical puzzle and pull. The harder you pull, the more your fingers are locked. When you relax and quit the resisting, the fingers are easily removed.

The stinkin thinkin that you don't now have everything you want, becomes the inhibitor to getting anything else additional that you desire. By living in the state of wanting, we sometimes forget and take for granted what we now have. Regardless of how little that may be which, is only a perception, it is the inhibitor to transform you into a state of receiving more. Be thankful.

After gratitude comes the **dream**. The more out of the box that your dreams are, the further away they are from being bogged down by gravity. Dreaming is actually the first law of manifestation; the other two are speech and action. You are the owner of your dreams. If you love them, nurture them, speak of them, and develop them, then you can have them come true. When your dreams become achievable mentally, focus on them and they will grow. Think in terms of being several levels above where your businesses are currently. If you want your dreams to expand financially, expand your ESP,

Emotionally, **S**piritually, and **P**hysically.

Next is the **plan**. Write down your goals and set deadlines. Make a chart that lists all of your daily and weekly accomplishments and milestones. Set a course for increasing your net worth for both the short term and the long term. List ten of the most important things to do and prioritize them.

This is not a should do, but a **must do** attitude. What you must do is have perseverance and dedication. Make yourself responsible and follow through, never giving up against the challenges that might present themselves.

Tough out the rough times. You can handle them. Just pick yourself up. Remember those valuable words of Winston Churchill,

"Never, never, never, never surrender, don't give up."

The more persistent you are, the more likely you are to succeed.

When you have planned your quest for success, forget about your comfort zones. Picture yourself boxed in a corner, and in order to get out you must activate your dream. Where is your sense of adventure?

Doing deals is enjoyable and very spiritual for me. I compare it to fishing. If I have one little hook in the vast blue sea and I get skunked, catching nothing, just having gone through the motions made it fun and okay. The experience of being there on the outskirts and rim of the earth overlooking ripples of the tranquil waters, I have found solace, reverence, and awe.

Now, when I feel a fish bite my little hook and I set him, my nerves go into overdrive. My heart beats like a drum roll as I'm reeling him in. Just before I can take him out of the water it's as if he knows this is his last chance for emancipation by breaking loose, but lo and behold, I land him. I then remove his scales, clean him, take him home, cook him to feed my family, make a blessing on him, and then we eat him. This completion is euphoric and beyond words.

This is no comparison between the fish I catch to the fish you purchase at a market. Those are usually raised in a hatchery and have soft flabby meat. The fish I catch in the wild was successful at survival of the fittest. He is more muscular from swimming faster. He has jumped on the golden opportunities that came his way in the form of his own prey, on which he has survived.

You too will get better and stronger, being more alert when the golden opportunities come your way. If you hesitate, they can disappear like a fat anchovy might swim away as though he had wings.

Yes, there is the element of stress and the lack of which makes you weak, flabby, and prone to more unnecessary stress. It manages to disappear somehow when you are having fun.

Let each and every moment bring you happiness and satisfaction. Life is an adventure. You will have many adventures and you will have bigger goals and bigger accomplishments.

Now, who wants to be a millionaire?"

Our whole room must have been wide-awake because all of us raised our hands. Marlen then squinted with his head on an angle in an accusatory expression and with a sarcastic tone of voice adding,

"Well, if you're watching that show on television, turn it off, and you'll have a chance to become one. In fact, turn off the T.V. Better yet, have your cable disconnected. Millionaires know this and this is about modeling them. They do not get together with other millionaires and sit around a television acting like sofa-spuds or zombies. They know you can't be doing deals and watching T.V. If there is something to be watched on T.V., pay someone else to watch it for you. Millionaires don't do what you can inexpensively pay someone else to do. We call those MWC's, or minimum wage chores.

When I was in school, I had to take subjects I wasn't very good at. I was forced to take exams in these subjects that I detested and when I failed them, I had to repeat them over and over until I got a passing grade. Why do you have to do well in something you hate?

In business, if there is a task needing to be done and it is something I hate doing, I hire someone who is good at it and loves doing it. Don't waste your time doing MWC's, particularly when you don't enjoy them. Rarely is anyone taught how to become a millionaire in school, nor even in college.

Preparing to become successful involves doing what successful people do. Okay, so they have a Rolls-Royce and they keep it spotless, full of oil, gasoline, and all the other necessary fluids, etc., which allow those cars to function well. So you have a Ford Taurus, but is it clean? Do you treat it like a Rolls? Successful people take good care of their cars and so do we. They appreciate the things they have and so do we. These are displays of gratitude and in order to have more, we must respect, appreciate, and be thankful for what we have.

When successful people want to buy something, they don't come out of pocket to do so. Before spending, they first anticipate what they will do next to procure the money to buy what it is that they want. Then, and only then, will they make such a purchase. It is an example of the exit strategy coming before the entrance.

Doing what successful people do will rub off on you. If you don't know any successful people, I suggest you meet some. Let's face it, if you sleep with dogs, you'll awaken with fleas. Don't get me wrong all of you canine lovers. I have three of them myself and I love them. At times, they even sleep with my wife and me.

Did you know that if one out of every five people you know is fat, there is a twenty percent chance that you too will be fat! Look at my staff and I. We are not fat and every one of us is successful while still growing, rich that is. You could make a good argument that having a large tummy is somewhat of a status symbol in this day and age. We want you to be healthy though, wealthy, and wise.

Ninety-six percent of the money in this country is controlled by five percent of the population. Sixty-five percent of all the money on this planet is controlled by one percent of the population. Don't try to re-create the wheel, do what the one percent do. Think outside the box.

When success falls into your lap accidentally, be wise, and nurture it. Serendipity is a cute word on which to fall back. It applies to these accidental rewards. This however is contrary to universal laws. When good fortune comes upon you serendipitously, and if that is your perception, beware. Easy come, easy go.

Achieving success is the final law of its manifestation. Whatever goes up must come down, may be a fallacy, at least when applied to extremes. There is a balance in nature and people who succeed are not always successful. In the process of planning, make sure to include what you will do when you reach your goals.

The phenomenon of success is the more you succeed, the more that will be expected of you. Do not be influenced by the pessimists, or even the optimists for that matter. Be happy. When you're on a roll, continue to be.

Spend less than you earn and invest the difference.

Each moment requires happiness and not just from achieving various goals. Too much pain leaves you without life's meaning.

Do things to help others. Add value to their lives. Mitigate their wants and needs.

Before we stop for a short break, I want to tell you that an hour with a good mentor can be more valuable and far less expensive than an entire college business course. Your mentors should understand your needs and want to help you avoid the pitfalls they have already personally encountered from their own successful business experiences.

Let's take a fifteen-minute break and please ask our staff to help you in any way.

We have some surprises for all of you, so make sure you get back in time.

CHAPTER 12

THE PASSIONATE KISS

Melky, Fred, and I remained in our seats, the three of us mumbling to each other about what we had learned while having obvious dialogues in our own minds. Marlen had a flock of people all around him. I then mentioned to the guys,

"These Marlen Gandalph groupies remind me of Hobbits from the shires of middle earth, possessing the ring of riches while on a quest through the passageways, to the voids of Hell, where they may cast the ring to end all evil."

Fred, had no idea what I was talking about which became revealed when he said,

"Who?"

Melky was laughing while telling us,

"Esther Malka, you never cease to amaze me. That was quite funny. I actually wouldn't mind being one of his groupies. I had this feeling all along that Marlen was a storehouse of information and was quite surprised to hear such altruistic viewpoints. What do you suppose will be the 50th passageway?

Fred guessed, "Bible study."

Melky said he had no clue but was eager to hear more. He still had that rose-colored aura around his face. I thought about asking him to spend the evening with me, only to talk with him and pick his brain. I nixed that idea, and anyway the man is supposed to pursue the woman, so I thought.

Fred mentioned to Melky that he felt there was a lot of Biblical implications in Marlen's teaching. Melky agreed but corrected Fred by saying they were spiritual and not necessarily Biblical.

"What's the difference?" Fred asked.

Melky and I simultaneously answered,

"You don't have to be religious to be spiritual"

He and I then both looked at each other, smiling. Fred then walked to the back of the room to talk with a staff member. I could tell that Melky was beginning to get engrossed in thought so I decided to make some small talk.

"Hey Melky, what's your favorite color?"

"Violet, why?"

"Just thought I'd ask."

"What's yours?"

"Red"

"Wow, we're connected"

"How is that? they're quite opposite."

"Exactly, we're both connected by pots of gold. Red and violet are the first and last colors of the rainbow spectrum."

"Interesting, I never really thought about that."

"Since we are on the subject of colors, what does white do for you?"

"Well, it's the combination of all colors and a symbol of purity. It's also the color of my panties."

"Very informative."

As Melky was about to continue, Marlen asked us all to take our seats and the 50th subject matter appeared on the power point screen.

Passageways to Riches #50
The Destination

"My friends, we are close to the end of this seminar. This will mark the first day of the beginning of the rest of your lives. 'Passageways to riches' are actually about more than money. You could have more money than you ever imagined and not be happy. You see, what riches are truly about, are having dreams, and whether or not you fulfill them, you can still have a rich destiny. Of course, we want you to be able to fulfill those dreams and we are here to teach you some of the details in how to bring them to fruition in the process of making tons of money.

A man once approached me and asked me in a very sad tone,

"I want to become rich and nothing I do seems to work. Every investment I have made has been a failure."

I asked him what was working out in his life. He said he does love his job. I then asked him what he does and he said he is a furniture mover. He added that his boss loves him and just gave him a small raise. I asked him to describe what he likes about his job. He told me he is appreciated. He said he can look at a room and almost instantly figure out how and when to move even large pieces of furniture, out of that room and into the company truck.

"It's not always so simple," he added. He said his boss calls him the engineer of the company.

I then asked him what else he's happy about in his life. He said he has a wonderful wife, Kathie, who appreciates practically everything he does and overlooks many of the foolish things he does.

Again, I asked him what else he's happy about in his life. He said he has three awesome kids, Heather, Kristen, and Marcus. He acknowledged he is proud of all three of them, they are all very smart, kind, and they are successful in many of their endeavors.

Again I asked him the same question. He said his company pays for his medical insurance and he just got back the results to a full physical exam. You guessed it, he's in perfect health.

There is no question that more is working well in his life but I then told him I recently went to visit a man who was one of the richest men in this country. The visit took place in a hospital where he was diagnosed having a rare and untreatable disease. I have known him for many years and he just went through a very ugly, drawn out, seventh divorce. He has four children from two different wives. Three of his children hated him and have not spoken to him in years.

I asked the furniture man if he would trade his life for my friend's life. He answered,

"No," with a smile on his face.

It's uncanny how we tend to forget or perhaps, take for granted what we have.

Riches, my friends, can be attained when you are grateful for the gifts and blessings that you have. Not being cognizant of what you have in your lives that are okay, will put barriers in front of you, inhibiting you from acquiring more.

Your destination is no enigma. If you want riddles, I might suggest the Farmer's Almanac. If you want mystery, read a novel. If you want to take unformulated chances, play the lottery. If you want a rich destiny, plan on it, smell it, taste it, feel it. There might be twists and turns like curveballs, screwballs, and change-ups, but as long as you're still playing, you'll get your share of hits and maybe even a home run every now and then.

Now tell me, what can you do to relieve society of its sadness, misery, poverty, war? It is easy to get caught up in money or in false recognition. If you are buying houses, how about buying every tenth house for the elderly or for the homeless. Have your CPA write it off.

Don't become lethargic. Stay sharp. Re-examine and realize that progress means change. Although subtle at times, businesses evolve.

Too much involvement in your businesses, even when you are doing well, can be stressful. By allowing a certain amount of entropy, happiness will accompany your success.

Find other interests and hobbies.

Take care of your bodies. Eat healthy foods, not just fast foods or half fast foods.

Exercise and take vacations with your loved ones.

Have a spellbinding future.

Realize your growth and your contributions.

Don't wait until your life is over to discover your particular meaning."

The PowerPoint projection on the screen then displayed a quote,

> *"Be fit for more than the thing you are now doing. Let everyone know that you have a reserve in yourself; that you have more power than you are now using. If you are not too large for the place you occupy, you are too small for it."*
>
> **—James Garfield**

"Live out your mission statement, and just what is your mission? Is there something spiritual about it? Are you about to help others or only yourself? These questions can separate success from failure.

Be well, be successful, and enjoy the ride."

Well everyone, our time here is up and I promised all of you a gift. Are you ready?"

The room screamed out,

"Yes!"

"Your present is the present."

After a long pause until Marlen started to laugh, he then explained,

"It's true. There's more. Everyone please stand up.

Face your neighbor and repeat after me.

I am worthy of my dreams."

Melky and I faced each other and we both repeated Marlen,

"I am worthy of my dreams"

Marlen added,

"Miracles are natural"

Smiling and somehow believing, Melky and I repeated this powerful statement and in sync with each other,

"Miracles are natural"

Neither Melky nor I could turn away from each other while Marlen spoke.

"Okay everyone; please sit back down and here is a gift we want to give you. We are going to take off half of the cost for our six-month boot camp, which guarantees you will purchase and sell at least one property and probably more. You will learn everything in detail that we touched on in this seminar. You will get 24/7 telephone hotline accessibility and two weekends of activating deals while in a seminar environment.

A wise carpenter once taught me you're only as good as your tools. Another wise carpenter taught me that you can do a lot of damage with fine tools if you don't know how to use them. This is what we do: We give you the tools and show you how to use them.

Folks, I can honestly say I love all of you. Never abandon the quest for love. It is defined as attention and not meant to diminish that very special concept. It is also the active choice to embrace and find satisfaction in this very process, which can take you to the extremities of pleasure.

Goodnight everyone."

The entire room went berserk with applause and when the roomful of people began to disperse, Marlen joined the staff in the back of the room to field questions and sign people up.

Melky smiled and his eyes, never going astray, just kept smiling at me. I smiled back and finally asked, "What? What do you want?"

After a brief pause, inquisitively, I looked at his throat throbbing. Hearing only silence, I said goodbye, turned around, and started to leave. He then managed to utter,

"What I want most is love."

I turned back around only to see him once again, grinning like a mule eating briars. I gave him my cell phone number and told him to call me.

I was wondering if Melky would call me. After listening to all of Marlen's positive thinking, which I now had engrained into my head, I wondered when Melky would call me. As I was leaving the seminar room, Melky approached the staff tables. I continued on, feeling somewhat lonely. Fred asked if he could take me back to Queens. I asked him if he wanted to walk around Times Square with me. He declined, saying that he would be reviewing the seminar information. He asked me if I would like to join him but I told him I had enough of the seminar for the weekend. I just wanted a peaceful walk in Times Square.

As I began my walk, I could not disregard many of Marlen's messages. I felt like I was grasping them on a different level, like using the other side of my brain, perhaps. I wanted to share this feeling with Melky and just that instant my phone rang.

Melky had Esther on his mind since Friday, from the first moment they faced each other. He was actually very shy around women, particularly with those that he wanted intimacy. He wanted to talk to her some more, at least to tell her the truth about what happened to him this weekend. More important though, he wanted to be with this attractive and interesting, Esther Malka. He knew deep down that he had a special connection to her. He finally left the staff table with Marlen and called her.

"Hello, is this Esther Malka?"

"Who were you expecting, Esther Williams?"

"Ah, the Olympic swimmer, funny you should mention her."

"Why is that?"

"Williams is the beginning of my last name."

"And what might that be?"

"Well, my stage name is Mel Williams."

"Get out of town!"

"Yep, Williams is short for Williamsberg."

"How did you wind up with Williamsberg for a last name?"

"When my Grandfather on my Father's side came to this country from Germany, before the First World War, he decided to create a secular first name, William, named after a former king and emperor. Berg was his real last name. Having poor English speaking skills, the customs agents assumed his last name was Williamsberg. His Hebrew name was Yosef, and so they wrote on his documentation, Joseph Williamsberg."

"Well, there's one for the books."

"Books, what books?"

"Why the law books, of course."

"What is that supposed to mean?"

"Haven't you ever heard of the case when a man shot an arrow at an apple above a child's head?"

"Well go tell it on the mountain."

"Mountain, why mountain?"

"A William he wanted to be. A fletcher like William Tell he never was. Berg however, translates as a mountain."

"Whoa, a little repartee from Melky."

"Actually, bantering is not one of my better skills."

"Well let's see what we could do about that. Humor is the spice of life."

"A gut buster, I'm not. Don't you think that life is funny enough?"

"Aw, come on, I seem to like your witty side as it stimulates scintillating conversation."

"Twinkling and sparkling are for the celestial bodies like the stars."

"Melky, I think you are a star. You even have a stage name. That reminds me, I noticed you seemed to be glowing, like you had a sunburn. The weather has been far from sunny. How did you get it?"

"It's a long story, but did you know that when it's overcast you're more prone to sunburn?"

"Yeah, right, listen, I'm on Broadway right now and I should probably get off the phone."

"Are you with Fred?"

"No, he left."

"Stay still for a minute. By the way, if it was perhaps possible, and I'm not saying that it is or isn't possibly possible, for it to be impossible to fall in love, would it be possible to just love and be loved, because I love talking with you and being with you. I have never met anyone who has so much to say, that says so much in such a small amount of time, and I love that too."

"Was that a question?"

"In a way but the real question is, will you have dinner with me tonight"

"Sure, Melky, when and where?"

"Where are you now?"

"I'm in front of the subway station on forty-second and Broadway."

"Be there before you can say Mr. Mxyzptlk."

I barely had the time to put on some fresh makeup and Melky arrived. He gave me a smile and a quick kiss then asked if I was ready. Foolishly, I answered,

"I'm always ready."

"I really like the smell of your perfume."

"Thanks, I'll tell you what it is if you'll buy me some."

"Sure, what is it?"

"I'm just kidding but I'm glad you like it."

Melky then flagged down a cab. About ten minutes later, we got out of the cab in front of a swank kosher restaurant in uptown Manhattan.

I happened to notice Melky paying the cabby and gave him a big tip. Melky seemed to be carrying a lot of money. Melky then took my hand and we walked inside the restaurant. Soon the maître d sat us down at a beautifully set table with a candle burning in the center of it. We each ordered a glass of wine and glanced over the menu. The lights were dim and the atmosphere was quite romantic.

When the wine was served, Melky made a blessing in Hebrew, which translated:

Blessed are you, Lord our G-D, king of the universe, who created the fruit from the vine. I answered, "Amen." We then took a sip. Melky smiled and asked me what I'd like. I told him I wasn't sure if it was on their menu. Still smiling, he said he was going to have the rack of lamb. I remarked,

"You really must like your sheep."

"I guess I'm a glutton for some mutton," he replied.

I then retorted,

"And I guess I'll abstain from the grief and have some boiled beef."

On their menu, it was called flanken, the Yiddish word for boiled beef.

It was a marvelous meal and we finished it with some coffee and chocolate mousse.

"Exactly what physical, mental, emotional, and spiritual desires do you have for your soul-mate?" Melky asked.

I hesitated, as he caught me off guard. I could only come up with the same question to him.

"What do you want from your soul-mate?"

He was quick to answer,

"From my better half I want a monogamous relationship. That much is a no brainer. When that is truly understood, neither of us will be jealous when the other is relating to someone else. Our relationship will be based on what is and not what should be. We will both know what the other one wants and if that changes, we will be willing to acknowledge it. We will both have the ability to listen to one another. When she is speaking to me, I will not own what she says to me. She will know that I am truly interested in what she has to say. From having such a high level of honesty between us, we will develop some telepathic abilities to know what the other one wants, but that will take some time. We will never threaten the other to end our relationship and we'll constantly seek ways to improve it and have more fun together. Rather than asking the other why, as in why did you do this or that, we'll replace it with what, as in what is it that you want to make the situation better. Since she is the number one in my life, I will give her what she wants, which she'll make clear to me. Whenever I can't give her that, I will be honest enough to tell her and seek something else that perhaps she'll accept in lieu of what I couldn't initially give her. I will have great satisfaction knowing I can give her what she wants and in a sense, I'll be doing that much for myself."

"Wow! It sounds like you really know what you want from your mate."

"And so do you, if you'll just take the time to organize your desires. It's a lot easier and beneficial to know what you want rather than hoping to get what you want. Tell him exactly what it is."

"I hear you Melky, and I can't speak for all women, but for me, there is a certain attraction to the mystique of inadvertently getting what I want from my man. I don't always want to have to tell him every single detail about what I want. I just want him to know, and I realize that could take some time. That might be the ESP of telepathy you were describing."

"I get it Esther, and speaking of time, a former band of mine is playing in Brooklyn tonight at a club called, Henry's Lounge. They usually ask me to sit in on a few tunes. Would you like to go check them out with me?"

"Sure," I answered.

I wasn't sure how I'd get back to Queens, but I felt confident that Melky would get me back to Anna's house safely.

We both said the grace after the meal and Melky paid the bill, again graciously leaving a large tip. As we walked outside, I thanked him for an enjoyable dinner. He said he hoped to have many more of the same with me. We only had to walk a block to the Brooklyn bound three train. When we got to that subway station, we walked down the stairs passing a wino blocking the stairway. He held out a hat and Melky dropped a ten-dollar bill in it. He thanked Melky and said,

"Bless you and the missus and have a wonderful evening."

Melky had a commuter pass, so we went right through the turnstiles and lo and behold, there was our three train waiting for us. That never happens to me. I usually just miss the train or have to wait, seemingly forever, which makes me nervous knowing there are all kinds of lowlifes down in these tunnels.

When we hopped aboard the train, we sat side-by-side and Melky turned to face me gazing into my eyes. I was motionless, feeling as though I was being seduced. Piece by piece, I could see him removing my clothes, slowly and one garment at a time. When I realized it was my own imagination, Melky held out his hand awaiting mine to take his. It was magnetic and I couldn't resist. We were conversing yet our lips never moved. We arrived at the Nevins Street station and exited the train. We walked holding hands. It felt so special. We had to walk about six blocks down 4th Avenue to Henry's Lounge.

We were in an Indian or Pakistani neighborhood having many stores that were closed then. It seemed that most of the stores sold trinkets, condiments, and books. I think this whole neighborhood was Islamic. It was quite dark out but whenever we crossed a street, we would look to the right, towards Manhattan, where lights were beaming from the skyscrapers and their reflection could be seen on the East River along with a sliver of the moon's crescent, which barely shed light onto itself. It was very dark and quite romantic.

As we crossed another street, Melky said that Henry's Lounge was just a block away. We simultaneously looked toward Manhattan again, crossing another street, only this time, falling from the sky, was a huge ball of fire. It was falling quickly and in a direction parallel to us on a slight angle over the East River. We both froze and when it passed our view, blocked out by old commercial buildings, Melky kept hold of my hand and we ran. Melky led us to an old corner building having a corner doorway with concrete columns and gargoyles on top of the columns. Melky said that we should be safe here in the strongest structural part of a building. We both assumed it was a large meteor. Both of us scared, Melky held his arms tightly around me as we anticipated the big explosion, if not doom. Melky put one of his hands above my head as if that would protect me while we waited for the explosion and its aftermath. We heard nothing, absolutely nothing but an eerie silence. We waited about five minutes, trembling there until a police patrol car slowly passed by. One of the two cops gave us a once over and Melky nodded to the cop while pulling my hand to walk with him.

Henry's Lounge was on the next corner. We walked into the place, which looked like a typical Brooklyn bar to me. Behind the bar, there was a television on with no sound coming from it. Melky and I were focused on the TV, waiting to see or hear something about the fireball we just saw. There must have been about fifty people there and all obviously, oblivious to the fireball. The bartender motioned to Melky and he said he'll have a double shot of Glenlivet. Melky looked at me and I could only move my lips to say,

"Same for me."

Melky's former band was on a break from finishing their first set.

When the bartender returned with our drinks, Melky asked if she could put the news on the TV. He gave her a generous tip and she obliged him. Waiting to hear something about the spectacle we saw, nothing came up other than one of Melky's former band members who approached us. Melky introduced us. It was the leader of the band, Bobby B. He was kind of a smartass, and with a sarcastic smile he asked,

"If I tell you that you have a beautiful body, will you hold it against me?"

"Absolutely not," I answered.

The rest of Melky's former band members came up to us, one by one. Before introducing me, he asked each of them if they heard anything about a meteor and then told them what we saw. Bobby B. then interrupted with,

"You two better lay offa that shit."

We then pounded down our drinks and gazed back at the TV. We were still dumbfounded. The band then started another set with Bobby B. announcing,

"A former band member, Mel Williams, might oblige us by sitting in on a song called, 'My Sweet Little Angel', whaddya say Mel?"

Melky looked at me, gave me a kiss, and then pulled a harmonica out of his pocket. He approached the stage to a microphone and joined in with the band. The song was a cross between a jazz and R&B tune. Melky was playing the rhythm on harmonica in the background while Bobby B. sounded really good playing guitar and singing. Soon, Bobby B. backed away from his mike and Melky began this awesome solo on harmonica while pointing to me. I started to blush and the fireball disappeared from my mind. Melky's harmonica riff was like nothing I ever heard before. It was amazing. After the song, Bobby B. asked for a round of applause for Mel Williams and Melky got a well-deserved standing ovation. Melky walked right back to me and I gave him a peck on the cheek. He smiled at me and said,

"Let's go."

While the crowd asked for more, Melky yelled out,

"Thanks, fellas," pointing to the band, and he marched me out the door with him. While leaving, I told him I liked his stage name. I asked him if he knew there was an area here in Brooklyn, also called Williamsburg. He told me it was spelled, b u r g, and his name was ...b e r g. An iceberg is what I was feeling like as we approached that corner building once again.

CHAPTER 13

THE PSYCHIC MENTOR
AND SUPER MENTEES

There was a man wearing a large white cape sitting in the exact same spot where Melky and I found shelter from the meteor explosion that never happened. The man held out a cup and Melky put a bill in it of some denomination. It was too dark for me to see how much it was.

"I am a psychic reader and I would like to give you a reading at no cost," he said. Without hesitation, he stood up, opened the door to the building, and stretched out his hand pointing inside for us to enter. Carelessly and without any thought of the possible consequences, we followed him in.

Earlier, I had the feeling that this building was condemned, blighted, or abandoned. The apartment, condo, or whatever it was, had a foyer with paintings of angels hanging on the walls. Beyond the foyer was a large living room furnished with ultra modern tables, sofas, and chairs. The living room was well lit with lighting that embellished his antique paintings and sculptures of angels. It looked as though he could have purchased them at the hotel art exhibit. He definitely needed a decorator because the combination of the artwork and his furniture created a mishmash motif. I sensed that he was eccentric and probably very wealthy. The furniture looked new and unused. It must have cost him a mint. The antique artwork looked priceless. Why then was he begging or holding out a cup for pittances?

He told us to make ourselves comfortable, holding out his hand pointing to a very modern white couch. We sat down noting that the couch looked like and felt soft as cashmere.

"I am Michel," he said with a French pronunciation.

He looked like he was Indian, Pakistani, or perhaps Arabic, speaking English with a foreign patois.

Melky began to introduce us but Michel interrupted, acknowledging,

"You are Esther Malka and Melchitzadek."

"How do you know our names?" I asked, beginning to feel alarmed.

"I am a psychic," he answered smiling, "However I also happened to hear you talking and playing music up the street."

"How could you hear us up the street?" I asked. Melky added,

"Nobody mentioned my full name up the street."

"Trust me when I tell you that I am psychic and I can actually hear thoughts from a long distance away. Did you enjoy the seminar?"

"How did you know we were at a seminar?" I asked.

"I am a psychic and you need to believe that," he answered, sounding very convincing

"We enjoyed it a great deal," Melky answered, before I could ask any more questions.

"Great deals are what the seminar appeared to be about, correct?"

Melky, looking inquisitive answered,

"Yes, but what do you mean by, appeared to be?"

"Everything is not always as it appears. Please allow me to explain. There are many messages to convey and I have only a short period of time to explain them to the two of you."

I was all ears at this point, now mildly distracted by the sweet fragrance of jasmine.

"Not only did you choose to attend the seminar, but you were chosen to attend. You have rare special powers that can be awakened. Your very names are symbolic of this."

Melky took a deep breath and sat back on the couch. Slightly terrified, I was sitting on the very edge of the couch, ready to bolt. I was side tracked though, smelling that sweet fragrance of actual jasmine. It didn't smell like incense. It smelled like real jasmine. I knew jasmine wasn't indigenous to this area nor did it grow anywhere near these parts in the concrete jungle of New York, so I quickly asked Michel,

"Do you happen to have a jasmine plant or have you been burning any incense?"

He smiled and then answered,

"No, but interesting that you should ask, Jasmine, pronounced, yasmin, is an Arabic word meaning gift from G-D. Now please pay close attention to what I must explain. The messages I will deliver are very important.

There is a seed germinating evil that you must learn about and come to understand. I was summoned here to find both of you. You possess a marriage of true minds that might make a difference."

"Marriage of true minds, isn't that is a quote from Shakespeare?

"Yes, and in your own words, why don't you explain it to Melky?"

"If I remember correctly, from a sonnet of Shakespeare, a marriage of true minds refers to the covenant between people bound by agreement or marriage having the power to defeat any adversary and overcome any obstacles in their path attempting to disrupt their covenant."

"That is why you two have been chosen. I must awaken your latent powers that can save humankind, the earth, and all of the species that dwell on your planet.

Melky scooted forward on the couch and looked at me asking,

"Who is this guy?" Michel then answered,

"I know you both better than you know yourselves. Your connection to the universe and to each other surpasses science and religion.

Your names are vessels." Pointing to me, he said,

"You were selected at birth and given the biblical name Esther Malka, meaning Queen Esther, one of the greatest saints as well as a prophetess. Through humility and prayer, she led a passionate plea that awakened the power to sustain and nurture an entire race of people. She became a Queen of the Persian Empire twenty-five hundred years ago, only because her identity, being an Israelite, was mistaken for that of a Babylonian. The Persians initially believed her name Esther, was related to Ishtar, the Babylonian goddess of fertility, love, war, and sex. Her name was actually Hebrew and derived from the root, Hester, meaning concealed or hidden. Her divine powers were revealed when the threat of genocide became apparent.

And you," pointing to Melky, he continued,

"You were selected at birth and given the biblical name, Melchitzadek, meaning righteous king. He was the king of a place called Salem. Salem means peace. That area later became Jerusalem, meaning peace will be seen. A king has a tradition of mercy as well as power.

Your desire to seek righteousness will empower you to be a master. Mastery is one of the prime ingredients needed to make peace. The other necessities to achieve peace are Presence, Gratitude, and Love. Our names, I mean your names are connected in the ancient language known as the Holy Tongue. Melech-king and Malka-Queen are names also connected to molach-salt, symbolic of preservation, and, Malach-a messenger or angel.

United, you will have compounding powers and will obtain more wisdom and understanding, which will transform into knowledge."

"Wait a second," Melky urged,

"Powers to do what?"

"This generation requires a superhero to save the world and its inhabitants."

Those were Michel's words, verbatim. Melky was so shocked his eyes looked like they were going to pop out of their sockets, I just chuckled and Michel kept speaking.

"G-D is the parent, watching His children damage His very own potential habitat. There is a concept that man must create a dwelling place for G-Dliness in this world. To do so, man must do some housekeeping. You must teach man to raise the bar on morality. A great deal of damage has been done to man's environment. Global warming, for example, has causes beyond just environmental abuse and neglect. Moral defilement has an even greater impact on the universe and all it contains. The moral laws that apply to all mankind, known as the seven Noahide precepts have been expurgated to benefit the perpetrators."

Curiously, I asked what he meant by expurgated and Melky was the quick one to answer.

"To expurgate is to edit and remove whatever you want in order to make something more palatable. If the Noahide laws have been expurgated, I would shudder to think about consequences."

Michel then asked Melky if he knew that the Noahide laws preceded Noah. Melky looked at me and answered,

"I would bet that Michel somehow knows I have lectured on environmental issues and spent a lot of time in seminary learning about our forefather, Noah, the builder of the famous ark.

There are six laws or precepts originally given over to Adam, the first man. They were all eventually violated by the masses and as a result, the great flood drowned all life other than those saved in Noah's Ark. The precepts were not necessarily in this particular order but:

1. There is a G-D.
2. Blaspheme is forbidden.
3. Murder is forbidden.
4. Theft is forbidden.
5. It is incumbent upon all of us to set up a just society.

6. Unnatural sexual activity is forbidden.

The seventh precept or law was added after the great flood, when Noah landed his ark.

7. You must not eat the flesh from a living animal; therefore, any form of animal cruelty is unacceptable."

When Melky said that, it reminded me that he was also an animal abuse investigator for the Humane Society. Michel asked him to describe the current state of the environment.

"Our physical environment is in a state of danger. If we do not change our ways, many species will suffer and possibly become extinct.

The United Nations set up a panel called the IPCC, or International Panel on Climate Control. There were over a thousand scientists that argued about how much of global warming is anthropogenic, meaning caused by man. Their findings created a debate over whether global warming was eighty percent or ninety percent man's fault. What's the difference?"

"Well spoken, Melchitzadek. Consider the current state of morality.

1. There is a G-D, yet idolatry is becoming more prevalent shown by those bowing down to drugs and other instant gratifications with no regard for the cumulative effects.
2. Blaspheme begins with man's slanderous speech towards his foes, then to his friends, then to his family, and then to his G-D.
3. Society is corrupted with unjust lawmakers and their enforcers. The scale of justice is grossly maligned and imbalanced.
4. Theft has become acceptable where the perpetrators are left unpunished. They take what they want and whenever they want, as though all is theirs for the taking with little or no regard to give anything back.

5. All forms of adultery, incest, rape, bestiality, and vile sexual activity are generated by all other forms of instant gratification with no understanding or concern about the cumulative repercussions.

6. Murder seems to resort and resolve differences of opinion. In your 20th century, over 100,000,000 people were murdered by their own fellow human beings.

7. The love and care for all species, which even include inanimate objects, are outweighed by the love of wealth and power.

Man has not learned the lessons of the great flood from Noah's time, which resulted in ELE's, Extinction Level Events. Those who resist the seven Noahide precepts will have negative fallout for generations after them, and that may be an optimistic point of view.

Amassing great fortunes is now the one and only concern.

Your world is threatened by evil and chaos, yet it is an essential part of G-D's universe imbued by the creator with potential for goodness and perfection. G-D is the connection between all that exists within the entire universe. G-D has given you the ability to transform your waste into energy for self-sustainment, without pollution, self-deprecation, or self-destruction."

"All right, I happen to agree, but what powers do we have and how do we use them?"

"You will develop and use them for the fight. Your main adversary is Lucifer. His name comes from the Latin, luz/light and ferre/bringer. The light he brings is dark. One challenge for your powers is to separate the devil and the deep blue sea. For there lies black gold, petroleum, a living entity safely contained in the bowels of Hades in wait of escape to pollute the waters in the sky and the waters below. Lucifer has created a plot to destroy life. That unkindest cut into the earth's crust, robs from the earth her black gold. Evil spreads from the decayed lands where the black gold has also been sought."

I flashed when he used the allusion, 'the unkindest cut,' and explained to Melky that he used a phrase once again from Shakespeare. Julius Caesar felt Brutus, his best friend, was his angel. It was Brutus who joined with an angry mob and stabbed Caesar, which was surely,' the unkindest cut' of all.

Michel then added, "Lucifer lies in wait while he sings the Sirens song, a song of deception, alluring the moneychangers to extract that which the planet needs to keep its waters and essentially its climates cool and lubricated. Lucifer is powerless when the black gold is kept confined. But, to the delight of Lucifer, when the oil is extracted from its natural containment, he will let it bleed into the waters, polluting them, and killing all sea life in its path.

The moneychangers will then transport the extracted oil to be burned for cooling and lubricating the machinations of man. Lucifer, the bringer of dark light, can then triumph by emitting his dark light through the sky, which will metamorphose into toxic black carcinogenic fumes. Everything that needs air to breathe will be choked. Those who elected to participate will not even take notice. They will be blinded by Lucifer's dark light.

Man is intelligent enough to understand how to use oil but not wise enough to know what it is used for in its far more important natural state. He happens to consume five times more oil than oxygen. Less important are the facts that the source for all oil will be depleted in about thirty years and soon it will cost more than gold. Time grows short for man to be weaned from this costly commodity. Irreparable damage has already been done and the worst is yet to come."

The analogies and allusions that Michel used made me feel like I was in a drama class within a gothic Daliesque setting. Melky sat there motionless; he seemed to be losing his attractive glow. When that caught my attention, I decided to ask,

"Who are you? And how on earth could we have been selected to have any powers to make a difference?"

Michel was silent for a brief moment, his eyes squinting, becoming very serious, answered,

"It doesn't matter who I am and it was not on earth where your destiny to be soul-mates was established. It was made in heaven. When you two will bond, as one, you will hear a voice, call it the universal consciousness, which will guide you and empower you to do that which you never thought possible. The two of you are destined to be together as one and you must not hesitate to live and love as one. You are extremely special soul mates. You should know that you are both spiritual in nature and natural in spirit. Your souls were destined to be together.

There are many battles to be fought against evil. There are other forces out there to join you on the side of good. The negative forces are however very powerful. You are both needed to join and lead those forces on the side of good to elevate mankind.

If mankind changes and improves its ways then the power of the external forces can be subjugated and the all-powerful forces of holiness will proliferate. Man could once again use his intelligence to elevate himself, the world, and much, much more than that.

It is known that you have both recently been less than cheerful. With a sorrowful heart, the spirit is depressed but a joyful heart makes for a cheerful countenance. The word for heart in the Holy Tongue is laiv, spelled lamed vet using the universal alphabet called Aleph-Bet. When you open up your hearts to each other, you will find the key to live and love eternally. A heart is like a fortress. As you learned at your seminar, a full heart expands and an empty heart struggles with great difficulty for acceptance."

Melky was glowing again and I suppose I was blushing. Could Melky have planned this matchmaking scene? It was too surreal. Melky then stole my heart saying,

"The signs I have been shown this weekend are uncanny and I don't question that I am in love with Esther Malka and I want to be with her. I also feel like this entire weekend has been a fantasy. What are you feeling Esther?"

"We have barely spent a weekend together. I do have strong feelings for you. My heart tells me that I love you and my mind urges caution to guard my frail emotions because my feelings have been hurt from past relationships. This weekend has also been a fantasy for me."

Michel then told us,

"Fantasies for some are realistic to others and realities for some are fantastic fantasies to others. You need to listen carefully and follow your heart. The window of time to act is short. Most things that you can think about for a lifetime you can do in an instant. Allow me to give you a glimpse into the future. Take each other's hand and rid your minds of all thoughts."

Melky and I glanced at each other, mentally coming to an agreement that there could be no harm in holding hands. With some trepidation we did so and Melky closed his eyes. I cautiously kept mine open until something very strange happened. A bright white light flashed, causing my eyes to close. Melky and I were at the altar. Everything that I saw thereafter was flashing in fast forward motion. We gave lectures to large groups of people, I wrote letters and articles, we travelled to many places while teaching others, we were in a hospital healing people, and then we were in a hospital where I was giving birth. It was a boy. Then I was in a hospital once again and this time I gave birth to a girl. Then the four of us were lecturing to scientists. We had a beautiful home that had elaborate furnishings. We seemed to have powers that were transforming the places we travelled into beautiful places where many people gathered. We went on many different missions to fight this apparent dark light. They looked scary but we never backed down from such adventures. In all of these visions, we were together and obviously happy. Michel then took our hands and separated them.

"Wow!" I exclaimed, that was awesome, all except the part where I am giving birth. Don't you think I'm a little too old for that?" Michel then answered,

"The original Melchitzadek blessed Abraham, Sarah, and all of their offspring. If you recall, Sarah gave birth to Isaac when she was in her late nineties.

Together you will be brought to the realization that you can have anything you want. The only boundaries and barriers are the doubts in your minds. Always keep your minds penetrable and open."

Melky seemed impressed with the vision he had and asked,

"What exactly should we do?"

"Your world is always on the brink of either Messianic times or massive destruction. One tip either way and all hope is either won or lost."

"Messianic times?" I asked.

"Yes, when the masses come to realize that they are all reincarnates having gone through a purification process. They will understand that now is their chance to do the greatest deeds they have always inherently wanted to do, since time immemorial."

"Why Messianic though?" I questioned.

"Because everyone has the potential to be Christ-like: kind to others where the only judgment is seeing the good in all. Within every living thing, there is a sacred microcosm and a world within itself. This is called the soul.

Currently, and for far too long, there has been the emotion of baseless hatred. It is a sin so grave that all of those around it are affected and the finality of death can be the result.

Every single small random act of goodness or kindness has the ability to create G-Dly light, transform an entire being, and that of the entire universe, the macrocosm.

Good health and well-being is available to all who take responsibility for their actions. Know yourselves, respect yourselves, love yourselves, love your neighbors, and do it now. There is but a fleeting window of opportunity. Universally it is but a blink of an eye. For you it is a lifetime. Time is moving faster now, particularly when truth and honesty are prevalent. Paradoxically you can now accomplish more. The masses are now more receptive of your powers to teach love and peace.

Learn how to convert negative situations into something positive. By teaching this, the masses will emit light, G-Dly light, and will be omitting the evil dark light of Lucifer."

"What situations," I asked.

"Negative situations present themselves, such as the time that Fred was late to take you to the seminar. You could have started an argument but instead of reacting negatively, you stayed focused on your goal, which was getting to the hotel. You got what you wanted. When serious negative situations present themselves, stay focused, turning them into something positive by being proactive instead of reactive. Isn't it better to be a cause for a good effect rather than being effected by a negative cause? It is simply a choice. Be on your guard for these situations. Appearing negative, they actually will offer an opportunity to create G-Dly light. When you create this light, people will be humbled by your radiance.

Your potential to educate and heal the world is unlimited.

The two of you will create a plan. Where there is no vision, people perish. As you proceed, you will grow stronger. You will speak to many and they that hear you will speak to many, having a positive rippling effect on the entire universe."

Melky was curious about the powers he saw in his vision. He asked,

"In my glimpse of the future I appeared to be powerful and felt super strong. What was that and how did I get that way?"

"By uniting, you will both become clairvoyant, hearing divine messages and be given the wisdom of Solomon. You will also gain the strength of Hercules. Your battles with evil will rarely require physical engagement, but there will come a time to defend yourselves. There are two of you and there is strength in numbers but beware of power, for power can destroy. Those that yield to temptation will succumb to it. If your motives are for the good, the Darth Vaders of your world will be held in check.

You will express power when speaking. You must also listen to and hear the others. Know where they are coming from. By your willingness to hear them, they will hear you. Of your five basic senses, four are paired, symbolic of their need to be used twice as much as speech.

ESP is a fallacy because there are no extra senses. You are one-hundred percent human beings. You will learn, practice, and teach the development of other senses, which may be perceived of as super-powers, and they must be carefully guarded. They will be used for healing, communication, travel, guidance, and anything meant for the purpose of doing good."

When Michel said that, I immediately felt like I was in a state of remembering something my soul already knew. That instant, Melky looked at me and grabbed my hand.

Michel continued, "You will teach man to once again use his intelligence to elevate the universe. You will bless him with the opportunity to change his ways just as a snake sheds his skin to become healthier and rejuvenated. Remind man of his many blessings, and that a blessing ignored can become a curse.

As rapidly, as a river flowing downhill, so too does wisdom. When this occurs, it begins to spew.

There is a voice crying in the wilderness. It is time for a Hail Mary to be thrown to the populace for the salvation of the multitude. You are the quarterbacks!"

Melky told me that a voice crying in the wilderness comes from the book of Isaiah, alluding to a lone protester whose warnings are ignored until it is too late. When he began to explain a Hail Mary pass, I told him that I had watched plenty of football with my three brothers and knew it was a desperation pass in a football game for an attempt to score.

"There is so much more that will come to you for the benefit of human existence. There will be obstacles, but essentially, once you take the first steps you will gain momentum. It will begin a perpetual motion.

To the angels you are a progeny descended from he who cast the original sin. Your reincarnations have evolved to the ultimate state of receiving the wisdom from the tree of knowledge. Our creator loves all children."

At that moment, I thought I was seeing daylight, believing that it was probably early morning. Michel told us that it was time for us to leave. I told him I had too many questions. His remark was,

"Listen to your questions, which is where you will find the answers."

He walked to the door, opened it and said,

"I envy you both and may your journey reach the ultimate enlightenment."

We walked outside where it was still dark. Melky looked into my eyes and asked,

"Can I hold you?"

"I certainly wish you would."

He put his arm around me and held me tight. I was trembling all the way to the next street. Melky then added even more surrealism.

"Esther, there is something I have wanted to share with you since Saturday."

"Okay, tell me the bad news."

"No, it's good news. I won an incredible amount of money in the lottery Friday night."

"Yeah sure, and I'm Superwoman."

"Well, apparently you are, or you will be, but I'm serious," he said with that Melky grin on his face.

"You won an incredible amount of money!" I repeated sarcastically.

"Pretty cool, huh."

"How did you do it?"

"Well, I had a fortunate feeling getting off the train after Friday's seminar. Meeting you reminded me of the book of Esther and the festival holiday of Purim. Purim means raffle or drawing of lots. I decided, thanks to you, to play six significant numbers in the lottery, which no one has won in over two months. I used the number eight, which is a symbol for completion in a refined world. I used nine, which is symbolic of the upper world or world of truth. Eighteen, for the numerical value of the word chai/ life. Twenty-six, for the Tetragrammaton and holy name of G-D, meaning I was, I am, and I will be. Then I used thirty-six for the lamed vav, or the hidden saintly ones known as the Nistarim. Then I chose thirty-nine, for all the tasks that were done in the Holy Temple, the thirty-nine books of the Tanach, our Bible, and the thirty-nine places in the Torah where it says we were strangers in a strange land and must teach our neighbors and have them as our friends.

It only cost me a buck."

"Unbelievable, why didn't you tell me sooner?"

"For starters, it was a blessing and I didn't want to upset it. I still can hardly believe it."

I wasn't sure who, but I thought of calling someone at that point, maybe to tell them about Melky's good fortune, only to realize I left my cell phone at Michel's. I told Melky and we agreed to walk back to Michel's place. He asked me not to tell anyone about his good fortune, still not wanting to alter his blessing. While we walked back to Michel's I asked Melky,

"What are you going to do with all the money?"

"Correction; What are we going to do with it. Why don't we use it for our mission to save the world? We could certainly travel anywhere to teach and donate to worthy charities."

That seemed like a great idea but then we got back to the building. We found my cell phone sitting in front of the door. We knocked and there was no answer. Then I noticed the door was nailed shut. There were no lights on and the whole building looked barren and blighted as it had when we first hid there. Melky shook his head and said,

"Let's go Esther, you said you liked mystique!"

After that, we were silent for about another block of walking towards the subway. We simultaneously looked up to the sky and saw a shooting star. We watched it ascend until it was out of sight.

Melky then knelt down on one knee and said,

"Esther, I know you think this is crazy but will you marry me?"

"Melky, this is crazy and I would have to be even crazier not to take notice of all the signs, so, yes I will marry you."

So began many adventures for the king and this queen to educate and unite a world full of subjects.